# CURSE OF THE MUMMY

# CURSE OF THE MUMMY

## VICTORIAN TALES OF ANCIENT EGYPTIAN TERROR

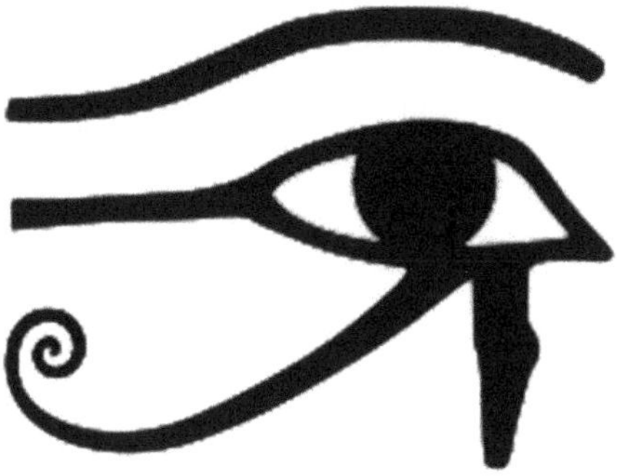

THIS ANTHOLOGY has been newly compiled, edited and typeset by Fox Editing for the Supernatural Fox Sisters' Supernatural History Series. The works were collected from various digital and print editions in the public domain and are presented unabridged. The original spellings have been retained, while some archaic punctuation has been lightly modernized.

COVER IMAGE: Seti I (d. 1279 BC), Egyptian pharaoh of the 19th Dynasty, New Kingdom and father of Ramesses II.
Albumen print by Émile Brugsch (AD 1842–1930) ca. 1881.
Museum of Egyptian Antiquities, Boulaq, Cairo.

CARTOUCHES: *Scarab with King as Bull Motif* and *Scarab with the Cartouche of Thutmose III*, ca. 1479–1425 BC.
Walters Art Museum, Baltimore.

EYE OF HORUS (*Wedjat*): Wikimedia Commons, CC BY-SA 4.0.

ISBN: 978-1-947587-05-2
First Trade Paperback Edition



Designed, typeset and edited by Katie Fox
foxediting.com • thesupernaturalfoxsisters.com

FOX
San Francisco

# CONTENTS

The Mummy's Foot
by Théophile Gautier ........................................... 1

After Three Thousand Years
by Jane G. Austin ................................................... 17

Lost in a Pyramid, or the Mummy's Curse
by Louisa May Alcott ......................................... 35

Lot No. 249
by Sir Arthur Conan Doyle .................................. 49

*The Authors* ......................................................... 93

*Let me gain the mastery over the great and mighty word*
*which is in my body in this place wherein I am,*
*for by means of it I will remember and I will forget.*

—The Egyptian Book of the Dead

# The Mummy's Foot

by Théophile Gautier

I HAD ENTERED, in an idle mood, the shop of one of those curiosity venders who are called *marchands de bric-à-brac* in that Parisian *argot* which is so perfectly unintelligible elsewhere in France.

You have doubtless glanced occasionally through the windows of some of these shops, which have become so numerous now that it is fashionable to buy antiquated furniture, and that every petty stockbroker thinks he must have his *chambre au moyen âge*.

There is one thing there which clings alike to the shop of the dealer in old iron, the ware-room of the tapestry maker, the laboratory of the chemist, and the studio of the painter: in all those gloomy dens where a furtive daylight filters in through the window-shutters the most manifestly ancient thing is dust. The cobwebs are more authentic than the gimp laces, and the old pear-tree furniture on exhibition is actually younger than the mahogany which arrived but yesterday from America.

The warehouse of my *bric-à-brac* dealer was a veritable Capharnaum. All ages and all nations seemed to have made their rendezvous there. An Etruscan lamp of red clay stood upon a Boule cabinet, with ebony panels, brightly striped by lines of inlaid brass; a duchess of the court of Louis XV nonchalantly extended her fawn-like feet under a massive table of the time of Louis XIII, with heavy spiral supports of oak, and carven designs of chimeras and foliage intermingled.

Upon the denticulated shelves of several sideboards glittered immense Japanese dishes with red and blue designs relieved by gilded hatching, side by side with enamelled works by Bernard Palissy, representing serpents, frogs, and lizards in relief.

From disembowelled cabinets escaped cascades of silver-lustrous Chinese silks and waves of tinsel, which an oblique sunbeam shot through with luminous beads, while portraits of every era, in frames more or less tarnished, smiled through their yellow varnish.

The striped breastplate of a damascened suit of Milanese armour glittered in one corner; loves and nymphs of porcelain, Chinese grotesques, vases of *céladon* and crackleware, Saxon and old Sèvres cups encumbered the shelves and nooks of the apartment.

The dealer followed me closely through the tortuous way contrived between the piles of furniture, warding off with his hand the hazardous sweep of my coat-skirts, watching my elbows with the uneasy attention of an antiquarian and a usurer.

It was a singular face, that of the merchant; an immense skull, polished like a knee, and surrounded by a thin aureole of white hair, which brought out the clear salmon tint of his complexion all the more strikingly, lent him a false aspect of patriarchal *bonhomie*, counteracted, however, by the scintillation of two little yellow eyes which trembled in their orbits like two louis-d'or upon quicksilver. The curve of his nose presented an aquiline silhouette, which suggested the Oriental or Jewish type. His hands—thin, slender, full of nerves which projected like strings upon the finger-board of a violin, and armed with claws like those on the terminations of bats' wings—shook with senile trembling; but those convulsively agitated hands became firmer than steel pincers or lobsters' claws when they lifted any precious article—an onyx cup, a Venetian glass, or a dish of Bohemian crystal. This strange old man had an aspect so thoroughly rabbinical and cabalistic that he would have been burnt on the mere testimony of his face three centuries ago.

"Will you not buy something from me today, sir? Here is a Malay kreese with a blade undulating like flame. Look at those grooves contrived for the blood to run along, those teeth set backward so as to tear out the entrails in withdrawing the weapon. It is a fine character of ferocious arm, and will look well in your collection. This two-handed sword is very beautiful. It is the work of Josepe de la Hera; and this *colichemarde* with its fenestrated guard—what a superb specimen of handicraft!"

"No; I have quite enough weapons and instruments of carnage. I want a small figure—something which will suit me as a paper-weight, for I cannot endure those trumpery bronzes which the stationers sell, and which may be found on everybody's desk."

The old gnome foraged among his ancient wares, and finally arranged before me some antique bronzes, so-called at least; fragments of malachite, little Hindoo or Chinese idols, a kind of poussah-toys in jade-stone, representing the incarnations of Brahma or Vishnoo, and wonderfully appropriate to the very undivine office of holding papers and letters in place.

I was hesitating between a porcelain dragon, all constellated with warts, its mouth formidable with bristling tusks and ranges of teeth, and an abominable little Mexican fetich, representing the god Vitziliputzili *au naturel*, when I caught sight of a charming foot, which I at first took for a fragment of some antique Venus.

It had those beautiful ruddy and tawny tints that lend to Florentine bronze that warm living look so much preferable to the gray-green aspect of common bronzes, which might easily be mistaken for statues in a state of putrefaction. Satiny gleams played over its rounded forms, doubtless polished by the amorous kisses of twenty centuries, for it seemed a Corinthian bronze, a work of the best era of art, perhaps moulded by Lysippus himself.

"That foot will be my choice," I said to the merchant, who regarded me with an ironical and saturnine air, and held out the object desired that I might examine it more fully.

I was surprised at its lightness. It was not a foot of metal, but in sooth a foot of flesh, an embalmed foot, a mummy's foot. On examining it still more closely the very grain of the skin, and the almost imperceptible lines impressed upon it by the texture of the bandages, became perceptible. The toes were slender and delicate, and terminated by perfectly formed nails, pure and transparent as agates. The great toe, slightly separated from the rest, afforded a happy contrast, in the antique style, to the position of the other toes, and lent it an aerial lightness—the grace of a bird's foot. The sole, scarcely streaked by a few almost imperceptible cross lines, afforded evidence that it had never touched the bare ground, and had only come in contact with the finest matting of Nile rushes and the softest carpets of panther skin.

"Ha, ha, you want the foot of the Princess Hermonthis!" exclaimed the merchant, with a strange giggle, fixing his owlish eyes upon me. "Ha, ha, ha! For a paper-weight! An original idea—artistic idea! Old Pharaoh would certainly have been surprised had someone told him that the foot of his adored daughter would be used for a paper-weight after he had had a mountain of granite hollowed out as a receptacle for the triple coffin, painted and gilded, covered with hieroglyphics and beautiful paintings of the Judgment of Souls," continued the queer little merchant, half audibly, as though talking to himself.

"How much will you charge me for this mummy fragment?"

"Ah, the highest price I can get, for it is a superb piece. If I had the match of it you could not have it for less than five hundred francs. The daughter of a Pharaoh! Nothing is more rare."

"Assuredly that is not a common article, but still, how much do you want? In the first place let me warn you that all my wealth consists of just five louis. I can buy anything that costs five louis, but nothing dearer. You might search my vest pockets and most secret drawers without even finding one poor five-franc piece more."

"Five louis for the foot of the Princess Hermonthis! That is very little, very little indeed. "'Tis an authentic foot," muttered the merchant, shaking his head, and imparting a peculiar rotary motion to his eyes. "Well, take it, and I will give you the bandages into the bargain," he added, wrapping the foot in an ancient damask rag. "Very fine? Real damask—Indian damask which has never been redyed. It is strong, and yet it is soft," he mumbled, stroking the frayed tissue with his fingers, through the trade-acquired habit which moved him to praise even an object of such little value that he himself deemed it only worth the giving away.

He poured the gold coins into a sort of mediæval alms-purse hanging at his belt, repeating:

"The foot of the Princess Hermonthis to be used for a paper-weight!"

Then turning his phosphorescent eyes upon me, he exclaimed in a voice strident as the crying of a cat which has swallowed a fish-bone:

"Old Pharaoh will not be well pleased. He loved his daughter, the dear man!"

"You speak as if you were a contemporary of his. You are old enough, goodness knows! but you do not date back to the Pyramids of Egypt," I answered, laughingly, from the threshold.

I went home, delighted with my acquisition.

With the idea of putting it to profitable use as soon as possible, I placed the foot of the divine Princess Hermonthis upon a heap of papers scribbled over with verses, in themselves an undecipherable mosaic work of erasures; articles freshly begun; letters forgotten, and posted in the table drawer instead of the letter-box, an error to which absent-minded people are peculiarly liable. The effect was charming, *bizarre*, and romantic.

Well satisfied with this embellishment, I went out with the gravity and pride becoming one who feels that he has the ineffable advantage over all the passers-by whom he elbows, of possessing a piece of the Princess Hermonthis, daughter of Pharaoh.

I looked upon all who did not possess, like myself, a paper-weight so authentically Egyptian as very ridiculous people, and it seemed to me that the proper occupation of every sensible man should consist in the mere fact of having a mummy's foot upon his desk.

Happily I met some friends, whose presence distracted me in my infatuation with this new acquisition. I went to dinner with them, for I could not very well have dined with myself.

When I came back that evening, with my brain slightly confused by a few glasses of wine, a vague whiff of Oriental perfume delicately titillated my olfactory nerves. The heat of the room had warmed the natron, bitumen, and myrrh in which the *paraschistes*, who cut open the bodies of the dead, had bathed the corpse of the princess. It was a perfume at once sweet and penetrating, a perfume that four thousand years had not been able to dissipate.

The Dream of Egypt was Eternity. Her odours have the solidity of granite and endure as long.

I soon drank deeply from the black cup of sleep. For a few hours all remained opaque to me. Oblivion and nothingness inundated me with their sombre waves.

Yet light gradually dawned upon the darkness of my mind. Dreams commenced to touch me softly in their silent flight.

The eyes of my soul were opened, and I beheld my chamber as it actually was. I might have believed myself awake but for a vague consciousness which assured me that I slept, and that something fantastic was about to take place.

The odour of the myrrh had augmented in intensity, and I felt a slight headache, which I very naturally attributed to several glasses of champagne that we had drunk to the unknown gods and our future fortunes.

I peered through my room with a feeling of expectation which I saw nothing to justify. Every article of furniture was in its proper place. The lamp, softly shaded by its globe of ground crystal, burned upon its bracket; the water-colour sketches shone under their Bohemian glass; the curtains hung down languidly; everything wore an aspect of tranquil slumber.

After a few moments, however, all this calm interior appeared to become disturbed. The woodwork cracked stealthily, the ash-covered log suddenly emitted a jet of blue flame, and the discs of the pateras seemed like great metallic eyes, watching, like myself, for the things which were about to happen.

My eyes accidentally fell upon the desk where I had placed the foot of the Princess Hermonthis.

Instead of remaining quiet, as behooved a foot which had been embalmed for four thousand years, it commenced to act in a nervous manner, contracted itself, and leaped over the papers like a startled frog. One would have imagined that it had suddenly been brought into contact with a galvanic battery. I could distinctly hear the dry sound made by its little heel, hard as the hoof of a gazelle.

I became rather discontented with my acquisition, inasmuch as I wished my paper-weights to be of a sedentary disposition, and thought it very unnatural that feet should walk about without legs, and I commenced to experience a feeling closely akin to fear.

Suddenly I saw the folds of my bed-curtain stir, and heard a bumping sound, like that caused by some person hopping on one foot across the floor. I must confess I became alternately hot and cold, that I felt a strange wind chill my back, and that my suddenly rising hair caused my night-cap to execute a leap of several yards.

The bed-curtains opened and I beheld the strangest figure imaginable before me.

It was a young girl of a very deep coffee-brown complexion, like the bayadère Amani, and possessing the purest Egyptian type of perfect beauty. Her eyes were almond-shaped and oblique, with eyebrows so black that they seemed blue; her nose was exquisitely chiselled, almost Greek in its delicacy of outline; and she might indeed have been taken for a

Corinthian statue of bronze but for the prominence of her cheek-bones and the slightly African fulness of her lips, which compelled one to recognise her as belonging beyond all doubt to the hieroglyphic race which dwelt upon the banks of the Nile.

Her arms, slender and spindle-shaped like those of very young girls, were encircled by a peculiar kind of metal bands and bracelets of glass beads; her hair was all twisted into little cords, and she wore upon her bosom a little idol-figure of green paste, bearing a whip with seven lashes, which proved it to be an image of Isis; her brow was adorned with a shining plate of gold, and a few traces of paint relieved the coppery tint of her cheeks.

As for her costume, it was very odd indeed.

Fancy a *pagne*, or skirt, all formed of little strips of material bedizened with red and black hieroglyphics, stiffened with bitumen, and apparently belonging to a freshly unbandaged mummy.

In one of those sudden flights of thought so common in dreams I heard the hoarse falsetto of the bric-à-brac dealer, repeating like a monotonous refrain the phrase he had uttered in his shop with so enigmatical an intonation:

"Old Pharaoh will not be well pleased. He loved his daughter, the dear man!"

One strange circumstance, which was not at all calculated to restore my equanimity, was that the apparition had but one foot; the other was broken off at the ankle!

She approached the table where the foot was starting and fidgeting about more than ever, and there supported herself upon the edge of the desk. I saw her eyes fill with pearly gleaming tears.

Although she had not as yet spoken, I fully comprehended the thoughts which agitated her. She looked at her foot—for it was indeed her own—with an exquisitely graceful expression of coquettish sadness, but the foot leaped and ran hither and thither, as though impelled on steel springs.

Twice or thrice she extended her hand to seize it, but could not succeed.

Then commenced between the Princess Hermonthis and her foot—which appeared to be endowed with a special life of its own—a very fantastic dialogue in a most ancient Coptic tongue, such as might have been spoken thirty centuries ago in the syrinxes of the land of Ser. Luckily I understood Coptic perfectly well that night.

The Princess Hermonthis cried, in a voice sweet and vibrant as the tones of a crystal bell:

"Well, my dear little foot, you always flee from me, yet I always took good care of you. I bathed you with perfumed water in a bowl of alabaster; I smoothed your heel with pumice-stone mixed with palm-oil; your nails were cut with golden scissors and polished with a hippopotamus tooth; I was careful to select *tatbebs* for you, painted and embroidered and turned up at the toes, which were the envy of all the young girls in Egypt. You wore on your great toe rings bearing the device of the sacred Scarabæus, and you supported one of the lightest bodies that a lazy foot could sustain."

The foot replied in a pouting and chagrined tone:

"You know well that I do not belong to myself any longer. I have been bought and paid for. The old merchant knew what he was about. He bore you a grudge for having refused to espouse him. This is an ill turn which he has done you. The Arab who violated your royal coffin in the subterranean pits of the necropolis of Thebes was sent thither by him. He desired to prevent you from being present at the reunion of the shadowy nations in the cities below. Have you five pieces of gold for my ransom?"

"Alas, no! My jewels, my rings, my purses of gold and silver were all stolen from me," answered the Princess Hermonthis with a sob.

"Princess," I then exclaimed, "I never retained anybody's foot unjustly. Even though you have not got the five louis which it cost me, I present it to you gladly. I should feel unutterably wretched to think that I were the cause of so amiable a person as the Princess Hermonthis being lame."

I delivered this discourse in a royally gallant, troubadour tone which must have astonished the beautiful Egyptian girl.

She turned a look of deepest gratitude upon me, and her eyes shone with bluish gleams of light.

She took her foot, which surrendered itself willingly this time, like a woman about to put on her little shoe, and adjusted it to her leg with much skill.

This operation over, she took a few steps about the room, as though to assure herself that she was really no longer lame.

"Ah, how pleased my father will be! He who was so unhappy because of my mutilation, and who from the moment of my birth set a whole nation at work to hollow me out a tomb so deep that he might preserve me intact until that last day when souls must be weighed in the balance of Amenthi! Come with me to my father. He will receive you kindly, for you have given me back my foot."

I thought this proposition natural enough. I arrayed myself in a dressing-gown of large-flowered pattern, which lent me a very Pharaonic aspect, hurriedly put on a pair of Turkish slippers, and informed the Princess Hermonthis that I was ready to follow her.

Before starting, Hermonthis took from her neck the little idol of green paste, and laid it on the scattered sheets of paper which covered the table.

"It is only fair," she observed, smilingly, "that I should replace your paper-weight."

She gave me her hand, which felt soft and cold, like the skin of a serpent, and we departed.

We passed for some time with the velocity of an arrow through a fluid and grayish expanse, in which half-formed silhouettes flitted swiftly by us, to right and left.

For an instant we saw only sky and sea.

A few moments later obelisks commenced to tower in the distance; pylons and vast flights of steps guarded by sphinxes became clearly outlined against the horizon.

We had reached our destination.

The princess conducted me to a mountain of rose-coloured granite, in the face of which appeared an opening so narrow and low that it would have been difficult to distinguish it from the fissures in the rock, had not its location been marked by two stelæ wrought with sculptures.

Hermonthis kindled a torch and led the way before me.

We traversed corridors hewn through the living rock. Their walls, covered with hieroglyphics and paintings of allegorical processions, might well have occupied thousands of arms for thousands of years in their formation. These corridors of interminable length opened into square chambers, in the midst of which pits had been contrived, through which we descended by cramp-irons or spiral stairways. These pits again conducted us into other chambers, opening into other corridors, likewise decorated with painted sparrow-hawks, serpents coiled in circles, the symbols of the *tau* and *pedum*—prodigious works of art which no living eye can ever examine—interminable legends of granite which only the dead have time to read through all eternity.

At last we found ourselves in a hall so vast, so enormous, so immeasurable, that the eye could not reach its limits. Files of monstrous columns stretched far out of sight on every side, between which twinkled livid stars of yellowish flame; points of light which revealed further depths incalculable in the darkness beyond.

The Princess Hermonthis still held my hand, and graciously saluted the mummies of her acquaintance.

My eyes became accustomed to the dim twilight, and objects became discernible.

I beheld the kings of the subterranean races seated upon thrones—grand old men, though dry, withered, wrinkled like parchment, and blackened with naphtha and bitumen—all wearing *pshents* of gold, and breastplates and gorgets glittering with precious stones, their eyes immovably fixed like the eyes of sphinxes, and their long beards whitened by the snow of centuries. Behind them stood their peoples, in the stiff and constrained posture enjoined by Egyptian art, all eternally preserving the attitude prescribed by the hieratic code. Behind these nations, the cats, ibixes, and crocodiles contemporary with them—rendered monstrous of aspect by their swathing bands—mewed, flapped their wings, or extended their jaws in a saurian giggle.

All the Pharaohs were there—Cheops, Chephrenes, Psammetichus, Sesostris, Amenotaph—all the dark rulers of the pyramids and syrinxes. On yet higher thrones sat Chronos and Xixouthros, who was contemporary with the deluge, and Tubal Cain, who reigned before it.

The beard of King Xixouthros had grown seven times around the granite table upon which he leaned, lost in deep reverie, and buried in dreams.

Further back, through a dusty cloud, I beheld dimly the seventy-two preadamite kings, with their seventy-two peoples, forever passed away.

After permitting me to gaze upon this bewildering spectacle a few moments, the Princess Hermonthis presented me to her father Pharaoh, who favoured me with a most gracious nod.

"I have found my foot again! I have found my foot!" cried the princess, clapping her little hands together with every sign of frantic joy. "It was this gentleman who restored it to me."

The races of Kemi, the races of Nahasi—all the black, bronzed, and copper-coloured nations repeated in chorus:

"The Princess Hermonthis has found her foot again!"

Even Xixouthros himself was visibly affected.

He raised his heavy eyelids, stroked his moustache with his fingers, and turned upon me a glance weighty with centuries.

"By Oms, the dog of Hell, and Tmei, daughter of the Sun and of Truth, this is a brave and worthy lad!" exclaimed Pharaoh, pointing to me with his sceptre, which was terminated with a lotus-flower.

"What recompense do you desire?"

Filled with that daring inspired by dreams in which nothing seems impossible, I asked him for the hand of the Princess Hermonthis. The hand seemed to me a very proper antithetic recompense for the foot.

Pharaoh opened wide his great eyes of glass in astonishment at my witty request.

"What country do you come from, and what is your age?"

"I am a Frenchman, and I am twenty-seven years old, venerable Pharaoh."

"Twenty-seven years old, and he wishes to espouse the Princess Hermonthis who is thirty centuries old!" cried out at once all the Thrones and all the Circles of Nations.

Only Hermonthis herself did not seem to think my request unreasonable.

"If you were even only two thousand years old," replied the ancient king, "I would willingly give you the princess, but the disproportion is too great; and, besides, we must give our daughters husbands who will last well. You do not know how to preserve yourselves any longer. Even those who died only fifteen centuries ago are already no more than a handful of dust. Behold, my flesh is solid as basalt, my bones are bars of steel!

"I will be present on the last day of the world with the same body and the same features which I had during my lifetime. My daughter Hermonthis will last longer than a statue of bronze.

"Then the last particles of your dust will have been scattered abroad by the winds, and even Isis herself, who was able to find the atoms of Osiris, would scarce be able to recompose your being.

"See how vigorous I yet remain, and how mighty is my grasp," he added, shaking my hand in the English fashion with a strength that buried my rings in the flesh of my fingers.

He squeezed me so hard that I awoke, and found my friend Alfred shaking me by the arm to make me get up.

"Oh, you everlasting sleeper! Must I have you carried out into the middle of the street, and fireworks exploded in your ears? It is afternoon. Don't you recollect your promise to take me with you to see M. Aguado's Spanish pictures?"

"God! I forgot all, all about it," I answered, dressing myself hurriedly. "We will go there at once. I have the permit lying there on my desk."

I started to find it, but fancy my astonishment when I beheld, instead of the mummy's foot I had purchased the evening before, the little green paste idol left in its place by the Princess Hermonthis!

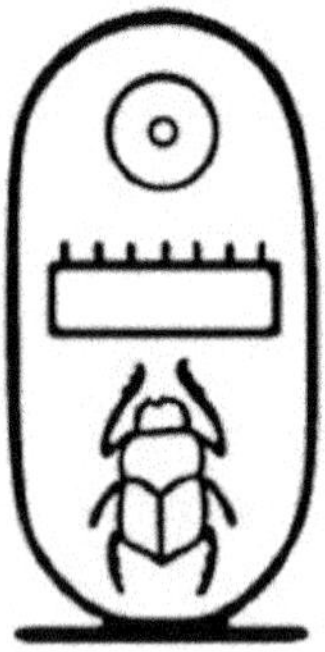

# After Three Thousand Years

by Jane G. Austin

"Do you remember the last request you made of me, when we parted in Paris, you to return homeward, and I to bury myself in the tombs of the Pharaohs?" asked Vance, the latest lion of Eastern travel, of Marion Harleigh, as he took her out to dinner at Madame Belletoile's.

"Perfectly. I asked you to bring me some personal ornament from the mummy of a princess," replied the young lady with sang-froid.

"And you promised to wear it, remember," pursued Vance, maliciously watching for the pallor that did not come.

"Exactly. I promised to wear it, and I am ready to keep my promise. Did you bring me the opportunity?"

"Could I have ventured to present myself before you without it?" replied the traveller, with smiling courtesy.

"And what is it?"

"May I come to-morrow, and offer it?"

"I shall be very glad to see you."

The next morning, at twelve o'clock, Vance rang at the door of Mr. Peter Harleigh's fine town-mansion, and, upon inquiring for Miss Harleigh, was shown at once to the drawing-room, graced by that young lady's presence. She came to meet him with outstretched hand.

"Welcome home!" said she, a little more earnestly, perhaps, than she would have spoken to Professor Byzantium, who also returned to New York from Eastern travel, by the Persia.

Millard Vance held the hand she offered, long enough to dart the piercing glance of his hazel eyes deep into the heart of the young girl, and then, releasing it, said softly,

"You are kind; but I have no home, you must remember."

"You should interpret the word more widely, and feel that your native land is enough for home, and your countrymen and women enough for family, at least in the present," said Marion, hating herself for the blush she could not restrain. Turning hastily, she added,

"This is Mr. Vance, Juliette. My cousin, Miss Randolph, Mr. Vance."

A little figure rose from the great arm-chair where she had been almost buried, and bowed smilingly in answer to the stately bow of the traveller. Then she seated herself upon the sofa beside Marion, and unconsciously offered her misty golden curls, pure complexion, and sweet blue eyes, in contrast to her cousin's trained and statuesque brunette beauty.

Vance, studying the two without looking at either, found it impossible to award the palm to either, and gave both credit for arranging a contrasting tableau—a manoeuvre for which Juliette was as yet too innocent, and Marion too proud.

After ten minutes, Vance drew a little Indian casket from his pocket and placed it in Miss Harleigh's hand.

"There is the Pharaonic spoil you have kindly allowed me to bring for you," said he.

Marion opened the box, and uttered a little cry of surprise. It appeared filled with golden beetles sparkling with phosphorescent gleams. Immediately she closed the lid upon them, and looked up into Vance's laughing face.

"They will not harm you; they are securely chained," said he, opening the case as it lay upon Marion's lap, and taking from it a necklace of golden scarabæi, with diamond eyes and green enamelled wings. Each insect was linked to each by a tiny chain, but so loosely as to admit of perfect freedom of movement. The necklace was clasped by a medal of burnished gold deeply graven with certain symbols or characters, not easily to be deciphered even as to form.

"Oh, the darling, lovely, odd thing!" exclaimed Juliette Randolph, while Vance lightly swung the glittering toy from his finger; but Marion turned pale, and slightly shivered.

"Where did it come from, Mr. Vance?" asked she.

"From the neck of a Pharaonic princess, as you desired that it should," returned Vance, watching with boyish zest the effect of his announcement.

"Oh, tell us all the story, please, Mr. Vance !—how you got it, and how she looked, and all," pleaded Juliette, settling herself in the sofa-corner with the impatient delight of a child about to listen to a fairy-tale.

Vance looked at her appreciatively, then suffered his regard to linger for a moment upon the proud, dark eyes Marion Harleigh had almost unconsciously fixed upon his own, before he gayly answered:

"Oh, yes; we travellers are but too happy in finding audience for our adventures, you know; and this one in a manner belongs with the necklace. I wintered upon the Nile last year, partly, no doubt, for my own pleasure, but partly, as I hope you will not refuse to believe, Miss Harleigh, in the hope of fulfilling your commission more certainly than a mere passing visitor could have done; for a new mummy is not to be met with every day, even upon the Nile; and I promised, you will remember, to take the ornament you were so kind as to ask for, directly from the person of its original possessor. My inquiries, bribes, false hopes, and opportunities of allowing myself to be cheated in the neatest possible manner, were unlimited; so also was my patience and my faith in its final reward. That faith was justified upon the day when my dragoman mysteriously introduced into the cabin of the Sphynx a rascally-looking Arab calling himself Sheikh of El Kab, the village off which we lay, and who offered for a compensation to conduct the illustrious lord, of whom he had heard as desirous of opening a new tomb, to the door of one discovered only a few days previously by himself and his son, who had resolved to sell their secret to the magnificent nobleman 'Inglis,' instead of to their own government, to whom it properly belonged.

"After hearing this story, I quietly remarked to my friend the Sheikh that I had been so many times imposed upon by the same account, and had lost so much time, patience, and money in consequence, that I had resolved to revenge myself upon the very next impostor for all that I had suffered at the hands of his fraternity, and that it was but fair to give him timely warning that I intended keeping to my resolution, and to offer him the chance of reconsidering his proposition.

"Without any pretence of being hurt in his feelings or wounded in his honor—pretences at which I should have only laughed—my Sheikh repeated his assertion that the tomb he mentioned was, and had been for ages, fast sealed, and that, from its situation and certain characters wrought upon the stone closing its door, he had no doubt it contained the remains of some person of consequence. Beyond this he knew nothing and professed nothing, and stipulated that, in all events, he was to receive a certain sum for admitting me to the tomb, let the results be what they might. Should they prove considerable, of course the reward was to be augmented.

"Rather impressed; after all, with the fellow's apparent honesty, I acceded to his terms, and that night, accompanied only by my two servants, I met him just outside the village, and followed to the catacombs perforating like the cells of a honey-comb the sandstone cliffs behind the town. The scene was wild enough, and more picturesque than you get even in the new Park, ladies; and, were I an artist either in words or colors, I would give it you with all the accessories of swarthy Arabs in snow-white drapery and turbans, flashing torches, gloomy subterranean passages, sculptured walls, and paintings yet glowing with all the richness of the original color. Sparing this, however, I will merely say that the old Sheikh proved himself a man of his word, and even 'builded better than he knew,' for the tomb whose door he had discovered hidden behind the pile of bones and dust half-filling an outer tomb, rifled ages ago, had never been opened, to all appearance, since it was first sealed up, perhaps three thousand years ago."

"Three thousand years!" softly exclaimed Juliette Randolph, opening her great blue eyes. "Has the world lasted more than three thousand years, Mr. Vance?"

Miss Harleigh's downcast eyes glittered impatient scorn; but Vance smiled with the indulgence rarely refused by men to a pretty woman's ignorance, while he replied,

"For perhaps four times three thousand years, Miss Randolph, woman's beauty and man's devotion have enacted upon this earth of ours the same old-new story that makes it today so beautiful and fresh, to fresh and beautiful eyes."

A little quivering smile emphasized the look not yet died out of Miss Harleigh's haughty eyes; but Juliette, blushing like a rose, lifted her innocent gaze to meet the meaning Vance rather looked than spoke, and then she said,

"But the story, Mr. Vance."

"Yes, the story. We penetrated the tomb at last, although not without much difficulty and hard work, for the cement was like stone, and the stone like—well, like stone itself. At last, however, we stood within the little chamber beside the single sarcophagus it contained. At the head lay, upon a sculptured pedestal, a lamp burned dry, but with the wick still clinging to the lip, and, at the foot, an exquisite vase of alabaster, three feet high.

"We lost no time, for the adventure was not without its peril had we been discovered by the Turkish authorities in opening the sarcophagus, and in removing the innumerable folds of mummy-cloth swathing the occupant by the expeditious means of slitting the whole series from neck to heel with a sharp knife, and turning it back like the covers of a box. Within lay a slight, elegant figure, very dark in color, as mummies nearly always are, but retaining sufficient beauty of outline, both in face and form, to prove to my mind that a rare loveliness of the days gone by lay before me, neither preserved nor quite destroyed; and in my heart I wished that the too careful love that had laid it here had rather given that beautiful form to Nature, who would in those three thousand years have produced and reproduced from that germ, flowers enough to beautify the whole earth.

"But Miss Randolph's eyes are exclaiming, 'The story! the story!' and I return, contritely. This mummy, I had expected, would be richly decorated with amulets and ornaments, for such was the rule in the interment of women of the higher class among the Egyptians; but, to my surprise, there was absolutely no ornament about it, with the exception of the necklace you now hold, and a small square box or reliquary of gold suspended from it and containing a bit of parchment enscribed with a brief hieroglyphic sentence. Carefully removing these, I folded the cerements once more about the silent figure, replaced the cover of the sarcophagus, and left my Pharaonic princess to resume the slumber I'd rudely disturbed. Let us hope that no evil dream connected with her lost necklace has marred her rest."

Vance ended smilingly; and Marion, who had listened with the utmost intentness, although never raising her eyes, suddenly looked at him, demanding,

"And what was written on the slip of parchment, Mr. Vance?"

"Hieroglyphics."

"But they can be read by modem science," replied Marion, a little impatiently.

"Yes; and the parchment, with an impression from the clasp of the necklace, is now in the hands of the man best qualified to decipher them, of all our cryptic scholars. I left them with him last night, and am to learn his decision today. You shall know it almost as soon as I."

"Thanks," said Marion, breathing a little more freely. "It would be horrible to me to have a three-thousand-year-old secret hung like a millstone about my neck, if I could never hope to solve it."

"Then you will wear the necklace?" asked Vance, smiling down upon her, for he had risen to take leave.

"Certainly. Shall you be at Mrs. Lane's tonight?" "May I hope to meet you there? We are going, and I shall wear the necklace of scarabæi, with many thanks to the giver."

"It is not a gift; it is a commission. You sent for it by me, as you send to Paris through your modiste for a new dress. It is a debt."

"Indeed!" exclaimed Marion, a little superbly. She had walked beside Vance the length of the drawing-room, and now stood near the door, out of ear-shot from the sofa.

"Yes," replied Vance, pausing in his leave-taking, and slowly adding,

"The price is already fixed. Do you wish to know it?"

"Perhaps I should know it before accepting the necklace. It may be beyond my means," said Marion, struggling for an indifferent look and tone.

"I think not—I hope not. I cannot tell you now what that price is,—but you will wear the necklace tonight?"

"Yes," murmured Marion, and felt glad to see him go.

"What a splendid man, Marion dear!—And he knows such a quantity! One really feels quite ashamed of ignorance beside him," prattled little Juliette; and her cousin, with a lingering, unfathomable smile upon her lips, made some vague reply, and hid the true answer in her heart.

That evening, at nine o'clock, came an imperative ring at the Harleigh door, and a message earnestly requesting Miss Harleigh to see Mr. Vance for one moment on important business.

In ten minutes she came down to him, superb in gold-colored silk and black lace, but without ornaments.

"Your business is very urgent, then, Mr. Vance," said she, a little haughtily.

"Thank God!" murmured Vance, staring at her regal neck and shoulders.

"For what? That you have some important business at last?" asked Marion Harleigh, one of the women who instinctively resent, even upon the man they love, the attempt to reconcile them to lure and jess. It was upon one of the profoundest truths of feminine nature that the mythologists founded their fable of Atalanta, of the sleeping princess—yes, of the Sphynx herself. He who approaches such a woman's heart with intent to win, must wholly subdue it, or she will turn upon him and slay him with her eyes for daring to make the attempt.

But Vance was too engrossed to note the antagonism so flattering to his vanity which had replaced Miss Harleigh's ordinary suavity.

"You have not put on the necklace!" exclaimed he at last.

"I was interrupted before my toilet was complete," said Marion.

"I can never be sufficiently thankful. I went from here to call upon the savant whom I mentioned this morning. He had gone out—as I afterward discovered, had gone to find me. I remained down-town, and finally dined at Delmonico's with a friend. On my way home I called once more upon the savant, whose first words were—

"Have you parted with that necklace?"

I said that I had presented it to the lady for whom it was procured.

"She will not wear it?" exclaimed he.

"She has promised to do so tonight," said I.

"Great Heaven! You have killed her, man!" thundered he, and then went on to show me the translation of the hieroglyph taken from the breast of the mummy. It was—

"See me, the beloved of a king. I scorned him for a lesser love, and thus I lie.'

"Upon the clasp of the necklace were engraved the words,

"'The gods who give life, also take it.'

"In some way that infernal (beg pardon, but I could not help it) necklace was the cause of that unhappy woman's death. Probably it is poisoned, and I—I brought it to you, and urged you to wear it—for my sake!"

His emotion was as unfeigned as it was evident; and Marion Harleigh forgot even her antagonism—forgot the danger she had escaped, and drooped her happy eyes, lest her lover should read them too easily.

But a lover reads his lady's eyes even through the lids, and, five minutes later, Millard Vance had presented Miss Harleigh with a girdle in place of the rejected necklace—a girdle formed of his own right arm; and she, her pride forgotten, submitted to its tender compulsion, nestled close to his heart, and even yielded her lips to his kiss, as meekly as the simplest country maiden could have done.

What wonder that Marion forgot then, or afterward, to repeat to any one the half-revealed secret of the necklace hidden in the depths of her well-stocked jewel-box?

The winter passed, and the spring, and Mr. Harleigh took his daughter, the niece who was to him almost another daughter, and the good-natured elderly cousin who matronized them, to the little cottage by the sea where they spent always a portion of the year.

Vance went also, finding quarters in a farmhouse close at hand, and spending all his time with the two girls. Marion, now that she had time to think and to command herself, was the most capricious and shyest of fiancées; and poor Vance never knew from day to day if he should be permitted to quietly lay his homage at her feet, or if he must watch to see it spurned, ridiculed, or rejected. Seldom, indeed, could he obtain a tête-à-tête and not unfrequently Marion declined altogether to see him, pleading, today a severe headache, tomorrow a dressmaker, the next day an imperative engagement in town, compelling her to leave with her father in the morning, not to return until his return at night.

In all his sufferings, at first poignant, but, alas I as time went on more endurable, from these various caprices and desertions, Vance found comfort always awaiting his acceptance in the pitying eyes and tremulous smile of Juliette Randolph, who, single-hearted darling that she was, could never understand how her cousin found pleasure in tormenting thus the man she loved—and such a man!

"Perhaps she does not love me, Juliette," suggested Vance, in disconsolate reply to this wonder, naïvely expressed on one occasion.

"Not love you, Millard!" Why, of course she does I How could she—" began the child, and there stopped, blushing like the dawn.

Vance, a master in heart-lore as in books, finished the sentence, read the blushing face, and his own grew suddenly pale. Then his gloomy eyes wandered across the sea to the horizon-line, and rested there so long, that Juliette, who had as yet guessed neither his secret nor her own, gayly asked of what he was dreaming.

"I was thinking what a pity I came home last winter," said Vance simply.

"Oh, don't talk like that! Marion will be well to-morrow, and perhaps gay and bright. And on those days, you know, you do not wish that you had not come home," said Marion's cousin, with a smile as tender as it was arch.

Vance glanced at her, then away, and, leading her back to the house, excused himself from entering, and spent half the night pacing up and down the beach with the wild sea breaking whitely at his feet.

"I must have an explanation with Marion; and, unless she will consent to an early marriage, I shall leave this for some time. I will travel again, or—"

But if the night brings counsel, it also puts to sleep and benumbs the counsel that came before; and when, next morning, Vance found his lady-love genial, beautiful, and even affectionate, he said nothing of the explanation or the journey, and the day went on as many a day had gone before.

And other days, and weeks, and months, while still the little party lingered at the shore, held by the warm, dry autumn days, as sweet as summer, and even richer in their gorgeous beauty.

And still the explanation had not come; and still Vance lingered; and still Juliette, the simple, loving child, all innocently sought to soothe the wounds inflicted by her haughty cousin, and all unconsciously gathered poison to herself from the wound she sought to heal.

At last there came a day when Marion, suddenly arraigning her own heart for judgment, found it guilty of hypocrisy, ingratitude, cruelty, and all uncharitableness toward the one creature upon earth for whose sake life was worth the living. She stood aghast at the record placed by memory before eyes too long and too wilfully blinded, and then took a resolve in strict accordance with her fault. As the sin had been a sin of pride, so the reparation was born of a profound and sweet humility,—child of pride wedded to love.

"I will go to him this moment," whispered Marion, "and, telling him bow dearly, how wholly I love him, I will beg forgiveness for my fault, and, if he wishes still to take me all to himself, I will—"

S0, on the moment she went. It was the night of the full moon, the harvest-moon, and all earth and ocean lay glowing and quivering in a bath of golden splendor. From the woods and fields came rich autumnal odors, and from over the sea, sighing breaths of a dying tropic breeze,—night-birds and insects on the one hand, the long waste of dreaming waves sliding up the sands, and breaking in music, upon the other. Marion stopped, to raise her face to heaven.

"Thank God for life, for this beautiful world, and for love," murmured she, and then went smiling on.

Her light feet made no noise upon the sand; the moon and the wind threw her long shadow and the rustling of her draperies behind her; and so she came all unconsciously along the beach to the spot where Vance and Juliette sat in the deep recess of a hollowed cliff.

Hearing her lover's voice, Marion paused. She could not speak indifferently to him just then, nor could she say what was in her heart to other ears than his. She hesitated, wondering how to act, but soon wondered no more, for Vance spoke again in answer to words which Marion did not hear.

"You do comfort me, darling; who else?" asked he passionately, and Marion, turned to stone as she stood, knew, as if she had seen it, the embrace and kiss that accompanied the words.

Then Juliette murmured sobbingly,

"Oh, Millard, you must not—you ought not! It is Marion whom you love, and she loves you. Let me go away from both of you—and die."

"No, you shall stay with me, and live," cried Vance, ardently." She does not love me now, if she ever did. Has not she been trying to prove how little she cares for me ever since we came here? And I—oh, darling, it is a simple, trusting, loving heart like yours that a man should give his own for. Marion is a splendid woman—a woman of grand intellect, passions, and possibilities; but you, Juliette, you are the dove whose nest is in my heart. Come to me, doveling—come to your home forever! Trust me; you have the right, and Marion will never suffer."

Then, in the pause that followed, she turned, and went her way, careless if she were seen and heard, or not. Turning her back upon the man that had wooed her to her doom, she saw her shadow stretching black and ominous along her path, and set her feet within it at every step. The dreaming sea, no longer whispering of love and hope, moaned wearily among its grasses; the sighing wind brought an odor of decay from the woods and fields, of chill unrest from the distant sea. The sands, that had seemed the golden dust of Pactolus, were of a sudden filled with flints and shards. All nature showed a change, and yet nowhere was change like that in the heart Marion Harleigh carried home from the little journey she had made to find her love.

The next morning Vance was awakened in the early dawn by the farmer's wife, who, standing at his bedside, laid a letter in his hand.

"It was brought by the Squire's man. He said you was to have it last night, but it was so late when he got here that we was all a-bed, and so he called again first thing this morning and made me come right up with it."

"Yes, thank you. That will do, Mrs. Brown," said Vance, who, holding the unopened letter, had turned of a sudden numb and chill, with a horrible, indefinite foreboding.

So soon as he was alone, he tore open the envelope with fingers almost too impatient and too tremulous to reach their object.

It contained the slip of parchment Marion had begged of him soon after their engagement, and a sheet of paper exhaling the violet perfume Marion loved, and with Marion's monogram at the top. It brought him this message:

"Your friend did not interpret the hieroglyph aright. This is my reading:

"Behold me, who fancied myself the beloved of a king among men. He scorned me for a lesser love, and thus I lie."

In ten minutes Vance, with death at his heart, was on his way to her who thus summoned him. The early morning was fresh and sweet and delicate in its beauty as a young girl's first dream of love, but Vance knew it no more than Cain, who fled from the wrath of God and the eyes of man with a brand upon his brow.

Arrived at the cottage, and finding only the servants astir, he ordered Marion's maid to go and ask if she could see him in half an hour.

The woman went, and, when her shrill shriek rang through the house, one listener at least was neither startled or doubtful of its meaning.

Striding up the stair, and past the frightened servant who ran to call her master, he entered the chamber alone, and stood beside the bed where lay his mistress, royal in death. She had dressed herself in the bridal robes, given her only a few days previously by her doting father, and magnificent in silk and lace and embroidery of oriental pearls. The bridal veil, fastened to her glorious corona of hair, swept down at either side, but no flowers encircled it, or lay upon the quiet bosom, or were clasped in the icy fingers. No flower, no jewel, no ornament of any description entered into that strange bridal toilet, save such as formed part of the dress itself, and a necklace of golden scarabæi about the throat.

With a groan, such as the rack might at last wring from the strongest heart, Vance bent to examine this necklace which had, as the merest glance showed, undergone some strange transformation.

Strange, indeed! The beetles, no longer mere toys and images, appeared to have suddenly assumed life, and the power attributed to them by the men who worshipped them as gods. Standing erect upon the myriad legs hitherto folded unobserved beneath their bodies with open wings, and upraised antennae, with their diamond eyes flashing and glittering in the first ray of the rising sun, the creatures appeared so fearful and so unearthly that Vance drew back a pace in terror from the sight. Recovering his manhood almost instantly, however, he snatched at the necklace with the shrinking hate of human nature in presence of the fiend, and would have torn it from its resting-place, although too late, for its work was done. But with a strange, new thrill of horror, he found the effort in vain. Each of these thread-like legs ended in a minute claw, and each of these claws, fastened deep in the flesh beneath, held to its prey, still warm beneath its deadly grasp.

The household, alarmed and wondering, were by this time flocking into the room; but Vance, turning upon them a pallid face, and strained, blood-shotten eyes, begged to be left yet a moment alone with the corpse of his promised wife. Only the father remained; and Vance, leading him to the bed, pointed at what lay there, saying, in a hard, cold voice,

"She dressed herself in these robes as a girl would naturally like to do, and she put this necklace about her neck. It was poisoned, as I told her when I gave it her, and warned her not to use it. She forgot my warning, and placed it about her throat, meaning, perhaps, to wear it as my gift when we should stand before the altar. I warned her, but she did not heed, and—there she lies."

Peter Harleigh, shrewd and crafty man of the world, looked long and earnestly into the face of his son-in-law, then into the face of the corpse, hardly sterner, hardly whiter, than that of the man; and at last he said,

"There is a mystery, but I do not care to fathom it, lest I hate the man my daughter loved. The story you tell will answer. Go, now, and leave me with my dead."

"I will take this; it is my right," said Vance, plucking away the necklace. Beneath it lay a livid band encircling the throat, and composed, as a close examination showed, of innumerable points or dots; but, even as they looked, this faded slowly from the surface, and, an hour later, the skin had become smooth and white as it had ever been.

No one saw Vance after this, until he stood with her father and cousin beside Marion Harleigh's open grave. When the services were ended, and the mourners, save themselves, dispersed, he turned to these two and simply said:

"Good-by. You will not see me again."

Juliette, uttering a faint moan, turned away; then, tottering, fell in a swoon like death.

Her uncle, pointing to her prostrate body, sternly met the eyes of the miserable man who stood staring gloomily before him, and said,

"Not her too, surely! Is not one enough?"

"If Juliette will marry me, you may set the day for yourself," said Vance, desperately.

"One year from to-morrow, if Juliette still wishes. Let my girl lie one year, one little year, in her grave first, and then her claims shall give way to those of the living," replied the old man bitterly; and Vance—

"One year from to-morrow I will come back. Then, if Juliette will marry me, she shall."

The year came round, and, with it, Vance. Juliette, who loved, and could not comprehend him, was ready to accept the sacrifice he offered instead of a heart, and they were married.

She is happy in her nursery and in her household, and she worships and deceives in a thousand little ways the husband she fears as much as she loves.

And he? Of his inner life we do not speak; of the outer let this fact suffice: where no eye but his own ever sees it, he hides a little Indian casket containing the Egyptian necklace. The scarabæi, no longer excited by contact with warm human flesh, lie in the quiescent state we first saw them, but the venom remains, the power remains; and Vance, looking at them, fancies often that they are but the outward symbols of the avenging memories that gnaw and sting his heart forever.

# Lost in a Pyramid, or the Mummy's Curse

by Louisa May Alcott

## I

"And what are these, Paul?" asked Evelyn, opening a tarnished gold box and examining its contents curiously.

"Seeds of some unknown Egyptian plant," replied Forsyth, with a sudden shadow on his dark face, as he looked down at the three scarlet grains lying in the white hand lifted to him.

"Where did you get them?" asked the girl.

"That is a weird story, which will only haunt you if I tell it," said Forsyth, with an absent expression that strongly excited the girl's curiosity.

"Please tell it, I like weird tales, and they never trouble me. Ah, do tell it; your stories are always so interesting," she cried, looking up with such a pretty blending of entreaty and command in her charming face, that refusal was impossible.

"You'll be sorry for it, and so shall I, perhaps; I warn you beforehand, that harm is foretold to the possessor of those mysterious seeds," said Forsyth, smiling, even while he knit his black brows, and regarded the blooming creature before him with a fond yet foreboding glance.

"Tell on, I'm not afraid of these pretty atoms," she answered, with an imperious nod.

"To hear is to obey. Let me read the facts, and then I will begin," returned Forsyth, pacing to and fro with the far-off look of one who turns the pages of the past.

Evelyn watched him a moment, and then returned to her work, or play, rather, for the task seemed well suited to the vivacious little creature, half-child, half-woman.

"While in Egypt," commenced Forsyth, slowly, "I went one day with my guide and Professor Niles, to explore the Cheops. Niles had a mania for antiquities of all sorts, and forgot time, danger and fatigue in the ardor of his pursuit. We rummaged up and down the narrow passages, half choked with dust and close air; reading inscriptions on the walls, stumbling over shattered mummy-cases, or coming face to face with some shriveled specimen perched like a hobgoblin on the little shelves where the dead used to be stowed away for ages. I was desperately tired after a few hours of it, and begged the professor to return. But he was bent on exploring certain places, and would not desist. We had but one guide, so I was forced to stay; but Jumal, my man, seeing how weary I was, proposed to us to rest in one of the larger passages, while he went to procure another guide for Niles. We consented, and assuring us that we were perfectly safe, if we did not quit the spot, Jumal left us, promising to return speedily. The professor sat down to take notes of his researches, and stretching my self on the soft sand, I fell asleep.

"I was roused by that indescribable thrill which instinctively warns us of danger, and springing up, I found myself alone. One torch burned faintly where Jumal had struck it, but Niles and the other light were gone. A dreadful sense of loneliness oppressed me for a moment; then I collected myself and looked well about me. A bit of paper was pinned to my hat, which lay near me, and on it, in the professor's writing were these words:

> *I've gone back a little to refresh my memory on*
> *certain points. Don't follow me till Jumal comes.*
> *I can find my way back to you, for I have a clue.*
> *Sleep well, and dream gloriously of the Pharaohs.*
> N N.

"I laughed at first over the old enthusiast, then felt anxious then restless, and finally resolved to follow him, for I discovered a strong cord fastened to a fallen stone, and knew that this was the clue he spoke of. Leaving a line for Jumal, I took my torch and retraced my steps, following the cord along the winding ways. I often shouted, but received no reply, and pressed on, hoping at each turn to see the old man poring over some musty relic of antiquity. Suddenly the cord ended, and lowering my torch, I saw that the footsteps had gone on.

"'Rash fellow, he'll lose himself, to a certainty,' I thought, really alarmed now.

"As I paused, a faint call reached me, and I answered it, waited, shouted again, and a still fainter echo replied.

"Niles was evidently going on, misled by the reverberations of the low passages. No time was to be lost, and, forgetting myself, I stuck my torch in the deep sand to guide me back to the clue, and ran down the straight path before me, whooping like a madman as I went. I did not mean to lose sight of the light, but in my eagerness to find Niles I turned from the main passage, and, guided by his voice, hastened on. His torch soon gladdened my eyes, and the clutch of his trembling hands told me what agony he had suffered.

"'Let us get out of this horrible place at once,' he said, wiping the great drops off his forehead.

"'Come, we're not far from the clue. I can soon reach it, and then we are safe'; but as I spoke, a chill passed over me, for a perfect labyrinth of narrow paths lay before us.

"Trying to guide myself by such land-marks as I had observed in my hasty passage, I followed the tracks in the sand till I fancied we must be near my light. No glimmer appeared, however, and kneeling down to examine the footprints nearer, I discovered, to my dismay, that I had been following the wrong ones, for among those marked by a deep boot-heel, were prints of bare feet; we had had no guide there, and Jumal wore sandals.

"Rising, I confronted Niles, with the one despairing word, 'Lost!' as I pointed from the treacherous sand to the fast-waning light.

"I thought the old man would be overwhelmed but, to my surprise, he grew quite calm and steady, thought a moment, and then went on, saying, quietly:

"'Other men have passed here before us; let us follow their steps, for, if I do not greatly err, they lead toward great passages, where one's way is easily found.'

"On we went, bravely, till a misstep threw the professor violently to the ground with a broken leg, and nearly extinguished the torch. It was a horrible predicament, and I gave up all hope as I sat beside the poor fellow, who lay exhausted with fatigue, remorse and pain, for I would not leave him.

"'Paul,' he said suddenly, 'if you will not go on, there is one more effort we can make. I remember hearing that a party lost as we are, saved themselves by building a fire. The smoke penetrated further than sound or light, and the guide's quick wit understood the unusual mist; he followed it, and rescued the party. Make a fire and trust to Jumal.'

"'A fire without wood?' I began; but he pointed to a shelf behind me, which had escaped me in the gloom; and on it I saw a slender mummy-case. I understood him, for these dry cases, which lie about in hundreds, are freely used as firewood. Reaching up, I pulled it down, believing it to be empty, but as it fell, it burst open, and out rolled a mummy. Accustomed as I was to such sights, it startled me a little, for danger had unstrung my nerves. Laying the little brown chrysalis aside, I smashed the case, lit the pile with my torch, and soon a light cloud of smoke drifted down the three passages which diverged from the cell-like place where we had paused.

"While busied with the fire, Niles, forgetful of pain and peril, had dragged the mummy nearer, and was examining it with the interest of a man whose ruling passion was strong even in death.

"'Come and help me unroll this. I have always longed to be the first to see and secure the curious treasures put away among the folds of these uncanny winding-sheets. This is a woman, and we may find something rare and precious here,' he said, beginning to unfold the outer coverings, from which a strange aromatic odor came.

"Reluctantly I obeyed, for to me there was something sacred in the bones of this unknown woman. But to beguile the time and amuse the poor fellow, I lent a hand, wondering as I worked, if this dark, ugly thing had ever been a lovely, soft-eyed Egyptian girl.

"From the fibrous folds of the wrappings dropped precious gums and spices, which half intoxicated us with their potent breath, antique coins, and a curious jewel or two, which Niles eagerly examined.

"All the bandages but one were cut off at last, and a small head laid bare, round which still hung great plaits of what had once been luxuriant hair. The shriveled hands were folded on the breast, and clasped in them lay that gold box."

"Ah!" cried Evelyn, dropping it from her rosy palm with a shudder.

"Nay; don't reject the poor little mummy's treasure. I never have quite forgiven myself for stealing it, or for burning her," said Forsyth, painting rapidly, as if the recollection of that experience lent energy to his hand.

"Burning her! Oh, Paul, what do you mean?" asked the girl, sitting up with a face full of excitement.

"I'll tell you. While busied with Madame la Momie, our fire had burned low, for the dry case went like tinder. A faint, far-off sound made our hearts leap, and Niles cried out: 'Pile on the wood; Jumal is tracking us; don't let the smoke fail now or we are lost!'

"'There is no more wood; the case was very small, and is all gone,' I answered, tearing off such of my garments as would burn readily, and piling them upon the embers.

"Niles did the same, but the light fabrics were quickly consumed, and made no smoke.

"'Burn that!' commanded the professor, pointing to the mummy.

"I hesitated a moment. Again came the faint echo of a horn. Life was dear to me. A few dry bones might save us, and I obeyed him in silence.

"A dull blaze sprung up, and a heavy smoke rose from the burning mummy, rolling in volumes through the low passages, and threatening to suffocate us with its fragrant mist. My brain grew dizzy, the light danced before my eyes, strange phantoms seemed to people the air, and, in the act of asking Niles why he gasped and looked so pale, I lost consciousness."

Evelyn drew a long breath, and put away the scented toys from her lap as if their odor oppressed her.

Forsyth's swarthy face was all aglow with the excitement of his story, and his black eyes glittered as he added, with a quick laugh:

"That's all; Jumal found and got us out, and we both forswore pyramids for the rest of our days."

"But the box: how came you to keep it?" asked Evelyn, eyeing it askance as it lay gleaming in a streak of sunshine.

"Oh, I brought it away as a souvenir, and Niles kept the other trinkets."

"But you said harm was foretold to the possessor of those scarlet seeds," persisted the girl, whose fancy was excited by the tale, and who fancied all was not told.

"Among his spoils, Niles found a bit of parchment, which he deciphered, and this inscription said that the mummy we had so ungallantly burned was that of a famous sorceress who bequeathed her curse to whoever should disturb her rest. Of course I don't believe that curse has anything to do with it, but it's a fact that Niles never prospered from that day. He says it's because he has never recovered from the fall and fright and I dare say it is so; but I sometimes wonder if I am to share the curse, for I've a vein of superstition in me, and that poor little mummy haunts my dreams still."

A long silence followed these words. Paul painted mechanically and Evelyn lay regarding him with a thoughtful face. But gloomy fancies were as foreign to her nature as shadows are to noonday, and presently she laughed a cheery laugh, saying as she took up the box again:

"Why don't you plant them, and see what wondrous flower they will bear?"

"I doubt if they would bear anything after lying in a mummy's hand for centuries," replied Forsyth, gravely.

"Let me plant them and try. You know wheat has sprouted and grown that was taken from a mummy's coffin; why should not these pretty seeds? I should so like to watch them grow; may I, Paul?"

"No, I'd rather leave that experiment untried. I have a queer feeling about the matter, and don't want to meddle myself or let anyone I love meddle with these seeds. They may be some horrible poison, or possess some evil power, for the sorceress evidently valued them, since she clutched them fast even in her tomb."

"Now, you are foolishly superstitious, and I laugh at you. Be generous; give me one seed, just to learn if it will grow. See I'll pay for it," and Evelyn, who now stood beside him, dropped a kiss on his forehead as she made her request, with the most engaging air.

But Forsyth would not yield. He smiled and returned the embrace with lover-like warmth, then flung the seeds into the fire, and gave her back the golden box, saying, tenderly:

"My darling, I'll fill it with diamonds or bonbons, if you please, but I will not let you play with that witch's spells. You've enough of your own, so forget the 'pretty seeds' and see what a Light of the Harem I've made of you."

Evelyn frowned, and smiled, and presently the lovers were out in the spring sunshine reveling in their own happy hopes, untroubled by one foreboding fear.

## II

"I have a little surprise for you, love," said Forsyth, as he greeted his cousin three months later on the morning of his wedding day.

"And I have one for you," she answered, smiling faintly.

"How pale you are, and how thin you grow! All this bridal bustle is too much for you, Evelyn," he said, with fond anxiety, as he watched the strange pallor of her face, and pressed the wasted little hand in his.

"I am so tired," she said, and leaned her head wearily on her lover's breast. "Neither sleep, food, nor air gives me strength, and a curious mist seems to cloud my mind at times. Mamma says it is the heat, but I shiver even in the sun, while at night I burn with fever. Paul, dear, I'm glad you are going to take me away to lead a quiet, happy life with you, but I'm afraid it will be a very short one."

"My fanciful little wife! You are tired and nervous with all this worry, but a few weeks of rest in the country will give us back our blooming Eve again. Have you no curiosity to learn my surprise?" he asked, to change her thoughts.

The vacant look stealing over the girl's face gave place to one of interest, but as she listened it seemed to require an effort to fix her mind on her lover's words.

"You remember the day we rummaged in the old cabinet?"

"Yes," and a smile touched her lips for a moment.

"And how you wanted to plant those queer red seeds I stole from the mummy?"

"I remember," and her eyes kindled with sudden fire.

"Well, I tossed them into the fire, as I thought, and gave you the box. But when I went back to cover up my picture, and found one of those seeds on the rug, a sudden fancy to gratify your whim led me to send it to Niles and ask him to plant and report on its progress. Today I hear from him for the first time, and he reports that the seed has grown marvelously, has budded, and that he intends to take the first flower, if it blooms in time, to a meeting of famous scientific men, after which he will send me its true name and the plant itself. From his description, it must be very curious, and I'm impatient to see it."

"You need not wait; I can show you the flower in its bloom," and Evelyn beckoned with the mechante smile so long a stranger to her lips.

Much amazed, Forsyth followed her to her own little boudoir, and there, standing in the sunshine, was the unknown plant. Almost rank in their luxuriance were the vivid green leaves on the slender purple stems, and rising from the midst, one ghostly-white flower, shaped like the head of a hooded snake, with scarlet stamens like forked tongues, and on the petals glittered spots like dew.

"A strange, uncanny flower! Has it any odor?" asked Forsyth, bending to examine it, and forgetting, in his interest, to ask how it came there.

"None, and that disappoints me, I am so fond of perfumes," answered the girl, caressing the green leaves which trembled at her touch, while the purple stems deepened their tint.

"Now tell me about it," said Forsyth, after standing silent for several minutes.

"I had been before you, and secured one of the seeds, for two fell on the rug. I planted it under a glass in the richest soil I could find, watered it faithfully, and was amazed at the rapidity with which it grew when once it appeared above the earth. I told no-one, for I meant to surprise you with it; but this bud has been so long in blooming, I have had to wait. It is a good omen that it blossoms today, and as it is nearly white, I mean to wear it, for I've learned to love it, having been my pet for so long."

"I would not wear it, for, in spite of its innocent color, it is an evil-looking plant, with its adder's tongue and unnatural dew. Wait till Niles tells us what it is, then pet it if it is harmless."

"Perhaps my sorceress cherished it for some symbolic beauty—those old Egyptians were full of fancies. It was very sly of you to turn the tables on me in this way. But I forgive you, since in a few hours, I shall chain this mysterious hand forever. How cold it is! Come out into the garden and get some warmth and color for tonight, my love."

But when night came, no-one could reproach the girl with her pallor, for she glowed like a pomegranate-flower, her eyes were full of fire, her lips scarlet, and all her old vivacity seemed to have returned. A more brilliant bride never blushed under a misty veil, and when her lover saw her, he was absolutely startled by the almost unearthly beauty which transformed the pale, languid creature of the morning into this radiant woman.

They were married, and if love, many blessings, and all good gifts lavishly showered upon them could make them happy, then this young pair were truly blest. But even in the rapture of the moment that made her his, Forsyth observed how icy cold was the little hand he held, how feverish the deep color on the soft cheek he kissed, and what a strange fire burned in the tender eyes that looked so wistfully at him.

Blithe and beautiful as a spirit, the smiling bride played her part in all the festivities of that long evening, and when at last light, life and color began to fade, the loving eyes that watched her thought it but the natural weariness of the hour. As the last guest departed, Forsyth was met by a servant, who gave him a letter marked "Haste." Tearing it open, he read these lines, from a friend of the professor's:

> DEAR SIR—*Poor Niles died suddenly two days ago, while at the Scientific Club, and his last words were: 'Tell Paul Forsyth to beware of the Mummy's Curse, for this fatal flower has killed me.' The circumstances of his death were so peculiar, that I add them as a sequel to this message. For several months, as he told us, he had been watching an unknown plant, and that evening he brought us the flower to examine. Other matters of interest absorbed us till a late hour, and the plant was forgotten. The professor wore it in his buttonhole—a strange white, serpent-headed blossom, with pale glittering spots, which slowly changed to a glittering scarlet, till the leaves looked as if sprinkled with blood. It was observed that instead of the pallor and feebleness which had recently come over him, that the professor was unusually animated, and seemed in an almost unnatural state of high spirits. Near the close of the meeting, in the midst of a lively discussion, he suddenly dropped, as if smitten with apoplexy. He was conveyed home insensible, and after one lucid interval, in which he gave me the message I have recorded above, he died in great agony, raving of mummies, pyramids, serpents, and some fatal curse which had fallen upon him.*
>
> *After his death, livid scarlet spots, like those on the flower, appeared upon his skin, and he shriveled like a withered leaf. At my desire, the mysterious plant was examined, and pronounced by the best authority one of the most deadly poisons known to the Egyptian sorceresses. The plant slowly absorbs the vitality of whoever cultivates it, and the blossom, worn for two or three hours, produces either madness or death.*

Down dropped the paper from Forsyth's hand; he read no further, but hurried back into the room where he had left his young wife. As if worn out with fatigue, she had thrown herself upon a couch, and lay there motionless, her face half-hidden by the light folds of the veil, which had blown over it.

"Evelyn, my dearest! Wake up and answer me. Did you wear that strange flower today?" whispered Forsyth, putting the misty screen away.

There was no need for her to answer, for there, gleaming spectrally on her bosom, was the evil blossom, its white petals spotted now with flecks of scarlet, vivid as drops of newly spilt blood.

But the unhappy bridegroom scarcely saw it, for the face above it appalled him by its utter vacancy. Drawn and pallid, as if with some wasting malady, the young face, so lovely an hour ago, lay before him aged and blighted by the baleful influence of the plant which had drunk up her life. No recognition in the eyes, no word upon the lips, no motion of the hand—only the faint breath, the fluttering pulse, and wide-opened eyes, betrayed that she was alive.

Alas for the young wife! The superstitious fear at which she had smiled had proved true: the curse that had bided its time for ages was fulfilled at last, and her own hand wrecked her happiness for ever. Death in life was her doom, and for years Forsyth secluded himself to tend with pathetic devotion the pale ghost, who never, by word or look, could thank him for the love that outlived even such a fate as this.

# Lot No. 249

by Sir Arthur Conan Doyle

Of the dealings of Edward Bellingham with William Monkhouse Lee, and of the cause of the great terror of Abercrombie Smith, it may be that no absolute and final judgment will ever be delivered. It is true that we have the full and clear narrative of Smith himself, and such corroboration as he could look for from Thomas Styles the servant, from the Reverend Plumptree Peterson, Fellow of Old's, and from such other people as chanced to gain some passing glance at this or that incident in a singular chain of events. Yet, in the main, the story must rest upon Smith alone, and the most will think that it is more likely that one brain, however outwardly sane, has some subtle warp in its texture, some strange flaw in its workings, than that the path of Nature has been overstepped in open day in so famed a centre of learning and light as the University of Oxford. Yet when we think how narrow and how devious this path of Nature is, how dimly we can trace it, for all our lamps of science, and how from the darkness which girds it round great and terrible possibilities loom ever shadowly upwards, it is a bold and confident man who will put a limit to the strange by-paths into which the human spirit may wander.

In a certain wing of what we will call Old College in Oxford there is a corner turret of an exceeding great age. The heavy arch which spans the open door has bent downwards in the centre under the weight of its years, and the grey, lichen-blotched blocks of stone are bound and knitted together with withes and strands of ivy, as though the old mother had set herself to brace them up against wind and weather. From the door a stone stair curves upward spirally, passing two landings, and terminating in a third one, its steps all shapeless and hollowed by the tread of so many generations of the seekers after knowledge. Life has flowed like water down this winding stair, and, waterlike, has left these smooth-worn grooves behind it. From the long-gowned, pedantic scholars of Plantagenet days down to the young bloods of a later age, how full and strong has been that tide of young, English life. And what was left now of all those hopes, those strivings, those fiery energies, save here and there in some old-world churchyard a few scratches upon a stone, and perchance a handful of dust in a mouldering coffin? Yet here were the silent stair and the grey, old wall, with bend and saltire and many another heraldic device still to be read upon its surface, like grotesque shadows thrown back from the days that had passed.

In the month of May, in the year 1884, three young men occupied the sets of rooms which opened on to the separate landings of the old stair. Each set consisted simply of a sitting-room and of a bedroom, while the two corresponding rooms upon the ground-floor were used, the one as a coal-cellar, and the other as the living-room of the servant, or scout, Thomas Styles, whose duty it was to wait upon the three men above him. To right and to left was a line of lecture-rooms and of offices, so that the dwellers in the old turret enjoyed a certain seclusion, which made the chambers popular among the more studious undergraduates. Such were the three who occupied them now—Abercrombie Smith above, Edward Bellingham beneath him, and William Monkhouse Lee upon the lowest storey.

It was ten o'clock on a bright, spring night, and Abercrombie Smith lay back in his arm-chair, his feet upon the fender, and his briar-root pipe between his lips. In a similar chair, and equally at his ease, there lounged on the other side of the fireplace his old school friend Jephro Hastie. Both men were in flannels, for they had spent their evening upon the river, but apart from their dress no one could look at their hard-cut, alert faces without seeing that they were open-air men—men whose minds and tastes turned naturally to all that was manly and robust. Hastie, indeed, was stroke of his college boat, and Smith was an even better oar, but a coming examination had already cast its shadow over him and held him to his work, save for a few hours a week which health demanded. A litter of medical books upon the table, with scattered bones, models, and anatomical plates, pointed to the extent as well as the nature of his studies, while a couple of single-sticks and a set of boxing-gloves above the mantelpiece hinted at the means by which, with Hastie's help, he might take his exercise in its most compressed and least-distant form. They knew each other very well—so well that they could sit now in that soothing silence which is the very highest development of companionship.

"Have some whisky," said Abercrombie Smith at last between two cloudbursts. "Scotch in the jug and Irish in the bottle."

"No, thanks. I'm in for the sculls. I don't liquor when I'm training. How about you?"

"I'm reading hard. I think it best to leave it alone."

Hastie nodded, and they relapsed into a contented silence.

"By the way, Smith," asked Hastie, presently, "have you made the acquaintance of either of the fellows on your stair yet?"

"Just a nod when we pass. Nothing more."

"Hum! I should be inclined to let it stand at that. I know

something of them both. Not much, but as much as I want. I don't think I should take them to my bosom if I were you. Not that there's much amiss with Monkhouse Lee."

"Meaning the thin one?"

"Precisely. He is a gentlemanly little fellow. I don't think there is any vice in him. But then you can't know him without knowing Bellingham."

"Meaning the fat one?"

"Yes, the fat one. And he's a man whom I, for one, would rather not know."

Abercrombie Smith raised his eyebrows and glanced across at his companion.

"What's up, then?" he asked. "Drink? Cards? Cad? You used not to be censorious."

"Ah! you evidently don't know the man, or you wouldn't ask. There's something damnable about him—something reptilian. My gorge always rises at him. I should put him down as a man with secret vices—an evil liver. He's no fool, though. They say that he is one of the best men in his line that they have ever had in the college."

"Medicine or classics?"

"Eastern languages. He's a demon at them. Chillingworth met him somewhere above the second cataract last long, and he told me that he just prattled to the Arabs as if he had been born and nursed and weaned among them. He talked Coptic to the Copts, and Hebrew to the Jews, and Arabic to the Bedouins, and they were all ready to kiss the hem of his frock-coat. There are some old hermit Johnnies up in those parts who sit on rocks and scowl and spit at the casual stranger. Well, when they saw this chap Bellingham, before he had said five words they just lay down on their bellies and wriggled. Chillingworth said that he never saw anything like it. Bellingham seemed to take it as his right, too, and strutted about among them and talked down to them like a Dutch uncle. Pretty good for an undergrad. of Old's, wasn't it?"

"Why do you say you can't know Lee without knowing Bellingham?"

"Because Bellingham is engaged to his sister Eveline. Such a bright little girl, Smith! I know the whole family well. It's disgusting to see that brute with her. A toad and a dove, that's what they always remind me of."

Abercrombie Smith grinned and knocked his ashes out against the side of the grate.

"You show every card in your hand, old chap," said he. "What a prejudiced, green-eyed, evil-thinking old man it is! You have really nothing against the fellow except that."

"Well, I've known her ever since she was as long as that cherry-wood pipe, and I don't like to see her taking risks. And it is a risk. He looks beastly. And he has a beastly temper, a venomous temper. You remember his row with Long Norton?"

"No; you always forget that I am a freshman."

"Ah, it was last winter. Of course. Well, you know the towpath along by the river. There were several fellows going along it, Bellingham in front, when they came on an old market-woman coming the other way. It had been raining—you know what those fields are like when it has rained—and the path ran between the river and a great puddle that was nearly as broad. Well, what does this swine do but keep the path, and push the old girl into the mud, where she and her marketings came to terrible grief. It was a blackguard thing to do, and Long Norton, who is as gentle a fellow as ever stepped, told him what he thought of it. One word led to another, and it ended in Norton laying his stick across the fellow's shoulders. There was the deuce of a fuss about it, and it's a treat to see the way in which Bellingham looks at Norton when they meet now. By Jove, Smith, it's nearly eleven o'clock!"

"No hurry. Light your pipe again."

"Not I. I'm supposed to be in training. Here I've been sitting gossiping when I ought to have been safely tucked up. I'll borrow your skull, if you can share it. Williams has had mine for a month. I'll take the little bones of your ear, too, if you are sure you won't need them. Thanks very much. Never mind a bag, I can carry them very well under my arm. Good night, my son, and take my tip as to your neighbour."

When Hastie, bearing his anatomical plunder, had clattered off down the winding stair, Abercrombie Smith hurled his pipe into the wastepaper basket, and drawing his chair nearer to the lamp, plunged into a formidable, green-covered volume, adorned with great, coloured maps of that strange, internal kingdom of which we are the hapless and helpless monarchs. Though a freshman at Oxford, the student was not so in medicine, for he had worked for four years at Glasgow and at Berlin, and this coming examination would place him finally as a member of his profession. With his firm mouth, broad forehead, and clear-cut, somewhat hard-featured face, he was a man who, if he had no brilliant talent, was yet so dogged, so patient, and so strong that he might in the end overtop a more showy genius. A man who can hold his own among Scotchmen and North Germans is not a man to be easily set back. Smith had left a name at Glasgow and at Berlin, and he was bent now upon doing as much at Oxford, if hard work and devotion could accomplish it.

He had sat reading for about an hour, and the hands of the noisy carriage clock upon the side-table were rapidly closing together upon the twelve, when a sudden sound fell upon the student's ear—a sharp, rather shrill sound, like the hissing intake of a man's breath who gasps under some strong emotion. Smith laid down his book and slanted his ear to listen. There was no one on either side or above him, so that the interruption came certainly from the neighbour beneath—the same neighbour of whom Hastie had given so unsavoury an account. Smith knew him only as a flabby, pale-faced man of silent and studious habits, a man whose lamp threw a golden bar from the old turret even after he had extinguished his own. This community in lateness had formed a certain silent bond between them. It was soothing to Smith when the hours stole on towards dawning to feel that there was another so close who set as small a value upon his sleep as he did. Even now, as his thoughts turned towards him, Smith's feelings were kindly. Hastie was a good fellow, but he was rough, strong-fibred, with no imagination or sympathy. He could not tolerate departures from what he looked upon as the model type of manliness. If a man could not be measured by a public-school standard, then he was beyond the pale with Hastie. Like so many who are themselves robust, he was apt to confuse the constitution with the character, to ascribe to want of principle what was really a want of circulation. Smith, with his stronger mind, knew his friend's habit, and made allowance for it now as his thoughts turned towards the man beneath him.

There was no return of the singular sound, and Smith was about to turn to his work once more, when suddenly there broke out in the silence of the night a hoarse cry, a positive scream—the call of a man who is moved and shaken beyond all control. Smith sprang out of his chair and dropped his book. He was a man of fairly firm fibre, but there was something in this sudden, uncontrollable shriek of horror which chilled his blood and pringled in his skin. Coming in such a place and at such an hour, it brought a thousand fantastic possibilities into his head. Should he rush down, or was it better to wait? He had all the national hatred of making a scene, and he knew so little of his neighbour that he would not lightly intrude upon his affairs. For a moment he stood in doubt and even as he balanced the matter there was a quick rattle of footsteps upon the stairs, and young Monkhouse Lee, half-dressed and as white as ashes, burst into his room.

"Come down!" he gasped. "Bellingham's ill."

Abercrombie Smith followed him closely downstairs into the sitting-room which was beneath his own, and intent as he was upon the matter in hand, he could not but take an amazed glance around him as he crossed the threshold. It was such a chamber as he had never seen before—a museum rather than a study. Walls and ceiling were thickly covered with a thousand strange relics from Egypt and the East. Tall, angular figures bearing burdens or weapons stalked in an uncouth frieze round the apartments. Above were bull-headed, stork-headed, cat-headed, owl-headed statues, with viper-crowned, almond-eyed monarchs and strange, beetle-like deities cut out of the blue Egyptian lapis lazuli. Horus and Isis and Osiris peeped down from every niche and shelf, while across the ceiling a true son of Old Nile, a great, hanging-jawed crocodile, was slung in a double noose.

In the centre of this singular chamber was a large, square table, littered with papers, bottles, and the dried leaves of some graceful, palm-like plant. These varied objects had all been heaped together in order to make room for a mummy case, which had been conveyed from the wall, as was evident from the gap there, and laid across the front of the table. The mummy itself, a horrid, black, withered thing, like a charred head on a gnarled bush, was lying half out of the case, with its claw-like hand and bony forearm resting upon the table. Propped up against the sarcophagus was an old, yellow scroll of papyrus, and in front of it, in a wooden armchair, sat the owner of the room, his head thrown back, his widely opened eyes directed in a horrified stare to the crocodile above him, and his blue, thick lips puffing loudly with every expiration.

"My God! he's dying!" cried Monkhouse Lee, distractedly.

He was a slim, handsome young fellow, olive-skinned and dark-eyed, of a Spanish rather than of an English type, with a Celtic intensity of manner which contrasted with the Saxon phlegm of Abercrombie Smith.

"Only a faint, I think," said the medical student. "Just give me a hand with him. You take his feet. Now on to the sofa. Can you kick all those little wooden devils off? What a litter it is! Now he will be all right if we undo his collar and give him some water. What has he been up to at all?"

"I don't know. I heard him cry out. I ran up. I know him pretty well, you know. It is very good of you to come down."

"His heart is going like a pair of castanets," said Smith, laying his hand on the breast of the unconscious man. "He seems to me to be frightened all to pieces. Chuck the water over him! What a face he has got on him!"

It was indeed a strange and most repellent face, for colour and outline were equally unnatural. It was white, not with the ordinary pallor of fear, but with an absolutely bloodless white, like the under side of a sole. He was very fat, but gave the impression of having at some time been considerably fatter, for his skin hung loosely in creases and folds, and was shot with a meshwork of wrinkles. Short, stubbly brown hair bristled up from his scalp, with a pair of thick, wrinkled ears protruding at the sides. His light-grey eyes were still open, the pupils dilated and the balls projecting in a fixed and horrid stare. It seemed to Smith as he looked down upon him that he had never seen Nature's danger signals flying so plainly upon a man's countenance, and his thoughts turned more seriously to the warning which Hastie had given him an hour before.

"What the deuce can have frightened him so?" he asked.

"It's the mummy."

"The mummy? How, then?"

"I don't know. It's beastly and morbid. I wish he would drop it. It's the second fright he has given me. It was the same last winter. I found him just like this, with that horrid thing in front of him."

"What does he want with the mummy, then?"

"Oh, he's a crank, you know. It's his hobby. He knows more about these things than any man in England. But I wish he wouldn't! Ah, he's beginning to come to."

A faint tinge of colour had begun to steal back into Bellingham's ghastly cheeks, and his eyelids shivered like a sail after a calm. He clasped and unclasped his hands, drew a long, thin breath between his teeth, and suddenly jerking up his head, threw a glance of recognition around him. As his eyes fell upon the mummy, he sprang off the sofa, seized the roll of papyrus, thrust it into a drawer, turned the key, and staggered back on to the sofa.

"What's up?" he asked. "What do you chaps want?"

"You've been shrieking out and making no end of a fuss," said Monkhouse Lee. "If our neighbour here from above hadn't come down, I'm sure I don't know what I should have done with you."

"Ah, it's Abercrombie Smith," said Bellingham, glancing up at him. "How very good of you to come in! What a fool I am! Oh, my God, what a fool I am!"

He sank his head on to his hands, and burst into peal after peal of hysterical laughter.

"Look here! Drop it!" cried Smith, shaking him roughly by the shoulder.

"Your nerves are all in a jangle. You must drop these little midnight games with mummies, or you'll be going off your chump. You're all on wires now."

"I wonder," said Bellingham, "whether you would be as cool as I am if you had seen——"

"What then?"

"Oh, nothing. I meant that I wonder if you could sit up at night with a mummy without trying your nerves. I have no doubt that you are quite right. I dare say that I have been taking it out of myself too much lately. But I am all right now. Please don't go, though. Just wait for a few minutes until I am quite myself."

"The room is very close," remarked Lee, throwing open the window and letting in the cool night air.

"It's balsamic resin," said Bellingham. He lifted up one of the dried palmate leaves from the table and frizzled it over the chimney of the lamp. It broke away into heavy smoke wreaths, and a pungent, biting odour filled the chamber. "It's the sacred plant—the plant of the priests," he remarked. "Do you know anything of Eastern languages, Smith?"

"Nothing at all. Not a word."

The answer seemed to lift a weight from the Egyptologist's mind.

"By the way," he continued, "how long was it from the time that you ran down, until I came to my senses?"

"Not long. Some four or five minutes."

"I thought it could not be very long," said he, drawing a long breath. "But what a strange thing unconsciousness is! There is no measurement to it. I could not tell from my own sensations if it were seconds or weeks. Now that gentleman on the table was packed up in the days of the eleventh dynasty, some forty centuries ago, and yet if he could find his tongue, he would tell us that this lapse of time has been but a closing of the eyes and a reopening of them. He is a singularly fine mummy, Smith."

Smith stepped over to the table and looked down with a professional eye at the black and twisted form in front of him. The features, though horribly discoloured, were perfect, and two little nut-like eyes still lurked in the depths of the black, hollow sockets. The blotched skin was drawn tightly from bone to bone, and a tangled wrap of black, coarse hair fell over the ears. Two thin teeth, like those of a rat, overlay the shrivelled lower lip. In its crouching position, with bent joints and craned head, there was a suggestion of energy about the horrid thing which made Smith's gorge rise. The gaunt ribs, with their parchment-like covering, were exposed, and the sunken, leaden-hued abdomen, with the long slit where the embalmer had left his mark; but the lower limbs were wrapped round with coarse, yellow bandages. A number of little clove-like pieces of myrrh and of cassia were sprinkled over the body, and lay scattered on the inside of the case.

"I don't know his name," said Bellingham, passing his hand over the shrivelled head. "You see the outer sarcophagus with the inscriptions is missing. Lot 249 is all the title he has now.

You see it printed on his case. That was his number in the auction at which I picked him up."

"He has been a very pretty sort of fellow in his day," remarked Abercrombie Smith.

"He has been a giant. His mummy is six feet seven in length, and that would be a giant over there, for they were never a very robust race. Feel these great, knotted bones, too. He would be a nasty fellow to tackle."

"Perhaps these very hands helped to build the stones into the pyramids," suggested Monkhouse Lee, looking down with disgust in his eyes at the crooked, unclean talons.

"No fear. This fellow has been pickled in natron, and looked after in the most approved style. They did not serve hodsmen in that fashion. Salt or bitumen was enough for them. It has been calculated that this sort of thing cost about seven hundred and thirty pounds in our money. Our friend was a noble at the least. What do you make of that small inscription near his feet, Smith?"

"I told you that I know no Eastern tongue."

"Ah, so you did. It is the name of the embalmer, I take it. A very conscientious worker he must have been. I wonder how many modern works will survive four thousand years?"

He kept on speaking lightly and rapidly, but it was evident to Abercrombie Smith that he was still palpitating with fear. His hands shook, his lower lip trembled, and look where he would, his eye always came sliding round to his gruesome companion. Through all his fear, however, there was a suspicion of triumph in his tone and manner. His eyes shone, and his footstep, as he paced the room, was brisk and jaunty. He gave the impression of a man who has gone through an ordeal, the marks of which he still bears upon him, but which has helped him to his end.

"You're not going yet?" he cried, as Smith rose from the sofa.

At the prospect of solitude, his fears seemed to crowd back upon him, and he stretched out a hand to detain him.

"Yes, I must go. I have my work to do. You are all right now. I think that with your nervous system you should take up some less morbid study."

"Oh, I am not nervous as a rule; and I have unwrapped mummies before."

"You fainted last time," observed Monkhouse Lee.

"Ah, yes, so I did. Well, I must have a nerve tonic or a course of electricity. You are not going, Lee?"

"I'll do whatever you wish, Ned."

"Then I'll come down with you and have a shakedown on your sofa. Good night, Smith. I am so sorry to have disturbed you with my foolishness."

They shook hands, and as the medical student stumbled up the spiral and irregular stair he heard a key turn in a door, and the steps of his two new acquaintances as they descended to the lower floor.

In this strange way began the acquaintance between Edward Bellingham and Abercrombie Smith, an acquaintance which the latter, at least, had no desire to push further. Bellingham, however, appeared to have taken a fancy to his rough-spoken neighbour, and made his advances in such a way that he could hardly be repulsed without absolute brutality. Twice he called to thank Smith for his assistance, and many times afterwards he looked in with books, papers and such other civilities as two bachelor neighbours can offer each other. He was, as Smith soon found, a man of wide reading, with catholic tastes and an extraordinary memory. His manner, too, was so pleasing and suave that one came, after a time, to overlook his repellent appearance. For a jaded and wearied man he was no unpleasant companion, and Smith found himself, after a time, looking forward to his visits, and even returning them.

Clever as he undoubtedly was, however, the medical student seemed to detect a dash of insanity in the man. He broke out at times into a high, inflated style of talk which was in contrast with the simplicity of his life.

"It is a wonderful thing," he cried, "to feel that one can command powers of good and of evil—a ministering angel or a demon of vengeance." And again, of Monkhouse Lee, he said,—"Lee is a good fellow, an honest fellow, but he is without strength or ambition. He would not make a fit partner for a man with a great enterprise. He would not make a fit partner for me."

At such hints and innuendoes stolid Smith, puffing solemnly at his pipe, would simply raise his eyebrows and shake his head, with little interjections of medical wisdom as to earlier hours and fresher air.

One habit Bellingham had developed of late which Smith knew to be a frequent herald of a weakening mind. He appeared to be for ever talking to himself. At late hours of the night, when there could be no visitor with him, Smith could still hear his voice beneath him in a low, muffled monologue, sunk almost to a whisper, and yet very audible in the silence. This solitary babbling annoyed and distracted the student, so that he spoke more than once to his neighbour about it. Bellingham, however, flushed up at the charge, and denied curtly that he had uttered a sound; indeed, he showed more annoyance over the matter than the occasion seemed to demand.

Had Abercrombie Smith had any doubt as to his own ears he had not to go far to find corroboration. Tom Styles, the little wrinkled man-servant who had attended to the wants of the lodgers in the turret for a longer time than any man's memory could carry him, was sorely put to it over the same matter.

"If you please, sir," said he, as he tidied down the top chamber one morning, "do you think Mr. Bellingham is all right, sir?"

"All right, Styles?"

"Yes, sir. Right in the head, sir."

"Why should he not be, then?"

"Well, I don't know, sir. His habits has changed of late. He's not the same man he used to be, though I make free to say that he was never quite one of my gentlemen, like Mr. Hastie or yourself, sir. He's took to talkin' to himself something awful. I wonder it don't disturb you. I don't know what to make of him, sir."

"I don't know what business it is of yours, Styles."

"Well, I takes an interest, Mr. Smith. It may be forward of me, but I can't help it. I feel sometimes as if I was mother and father to my young gentlemen. It all falls on me when things go wrong and the relations come. But Mr. Bellingham, sir. I want to know what it is that walks about his room sometimes when he's out and when the door's locked on the outside."

"Eh? you're talking nonsense, Styles."

"Maybe so, sir; but I heard it more'n once with my own ears."

"Rubbish, Styles."

"Very good, sir. You'll ring the bell if you want me."

Abercrombie Smith gave little heed to the gossip of the old man-servant, but a small incident occurred a few days later which left an unpleasant effect upon his mind, and brought the words of Styles forcibly to his memory.

Bellingham had come up to see him late one night, and was entertaining him with an interesting account of the rock tombs of Beni Hassan in Upper Egypt, when Smith, whose hearing was remarkably acute, distinctly heard the sound of a door opening on the landing below.

"There's some fellow gone in or out of your room," he remarked.

Bellingham sprang up and stood helpless for a moment, with the expression of a man who is half-incredulous and half-afraid.

"I surely locked it. I am almost positive that I locked it," he stammered. "No one could have opened it."

"Why, I hear someone coming up the steps now," said Smith.

Bellingham rushed out through the door, slammed it loudly behind him, and hurried down the stairs. About half-way down Smith heard him stop, and thought he caught the sound of whispering. A moment later the door beneath him shut, a key creaked in a lock, and Bellingham, with beads of moisture upon his pale face, ascended the stairs once more, and re-entered the room.

"It's all right," he said, throwing himself down in a chair. "It was that fool of a dog. He had pushed the door open. I don't know how I came to forget to lock it."

"I didn't know you kept a dog," said Smith, looking very thoughtfully at the disturbed face of his companion.

"Yes, I haven't had him long. I must get rid of him. He's a great nuisance."

"He must be, if you find it so hard to shut him up. I should have thought that shutting the door would have been enough, without locking it."

"I want to prevent old Styles from letting him out. He's of some value, you know, and it would be awkward to lose him."

"I am a bit of a dog-fancier myself," said Smith, still gazing hard at his companion from the corner of his eyes. "Perhaps you'll let me have a look at it."

"Certainly. But I am afraid it cannot be tonight; I have an appointment. Is that clock right? Then I am a quarter of an hour late already. You'll excuse me, I am sure."

He picked up his cap and hurried from the room. In spite of his appointment, Smith heard him re-enter his own chamber and lock his door upon the inside.

This interview left a disagreeable impression upon the medical student's mind. Bellingham had lied to him, and lied so clumsily that it looked as if he had desperate reasons for concealing the truth. Smith knew that his neighbour had no dog. He knew, also, that the step which he had heard upon the stairs was not the step of an animal. But if it were not, then what could it be? There was old Style's statement about the something which used to pace the room at times when the owner was absent. Could it be a woman? Smith rather inclined to the view. If so, it would mean disgrace and expulsion to Bellingham if it were discovered by the authorities, so that his anxiety and falsehoods might be accounted for. And yet it was inconceivable that an undergraduate could keep a woman in his rooms without being instantly detected. Be the explanation what it might, there was something ugly about it, and Smith determined, as he turned to his books, to discourage all further attempts at intimacy on the part of his soft-spoken and ill-favoured neighbour.

But his work was destined to interruption that night. He had hardly caught up the broken threads when a firm, heavy footfall came three steps at a time from below, and Hastie, in blazer and flannels, burst into the room.

"Still at it!" said he, plumping down into his wonted arm-chair. "What a chap you are to stew! I believe an earthquake might come and knock Oxford into a cocked hat, and you would sit perfectly placid with your books among the ruins. However, I won't bore you long. Three whiffs of baccy, and I am off."

"What's the news, then?" asked Smith, cramming a plug of bird's-eye into his briar with his forefinger.

"Nothing very much. Wilson made 70 for the freshmen against the eleven. They say that they will play him instead of Buddicomb, for Buddicomb is clean off colour. He used to be able to bowl a little, but it's nothing but half-volleys and long hops now."

"Medium right," suggested Smith, with the intense gravity which comes upon a varsity man when he speaks of athletics.

"Inclining to fast, with a work from leg. Comes with the arm about three inches or so. He used to be nasty on a wet wicket. Oh, by the way, have you heard about Long Norton?"

"What's that?"

"He's been attacked."

"Attacked?"

"Yes, just as he was turning out of the High Street, and within a hundred yards of the gate of Old's."

"But who——"

"Ah, that's the rub! If you said 'what,' you would be more grammatical. Norton swears that it was not human, and, indeed, from the scratches on his throat, I should be inclined to agree with him."

"What, then? Have we come down to spooks?"

Abercrombie Smith puffed his scientific contempt.

"Well, no; I don't think that is quite the idea, either. I am inclined to think that if any showman has lost a great ape lately, and the brute is in these parts, a jury would find a true bill against it. Norton passes that way every night, you know, about the same hour. There's a tree that hangs low over the path—the big elm from Rainy's garden. Norton thinks the thing dropped on him out of the tree. Anyhow, he was nearly strangled by two arms, which, he says, were as strong and as thin as steel bands. He saw nothing; only those beastly arms that tightened and tightened on him. He yelled his head nearly off, and a couple of chaps came running, and the thing went over the wall like a cat. He never got a fair sight of it the whole time. It gave Norton a shake up, I can tell you. I tell him it has been as good as a change at the seaside for him."

"A garrotter, most likely," said Smith.

"Very possibly. Norton says not; but we don't mind what he says. The garrotter had long nails, and was pretty smart at swinging himself over walls. By the way, your beautiful neighbour would be pleased if he heard about it. He had a grudge against Norton, and he's not a man, from what I know of him, to forget his little debts. But hallo, old chap, what have you got in your noddle?"

"Nothing," Smith answered, curtly.

He had started in his chair, and the look had flashed over his face which comes upon a man who is struck suddenly by some unpleasant idea.

"You looked as if something I had said had taken you on the raw. By the way, you have made the acquaintance of Master B. since I looked in last, have you not? Young Monkhouse Lee told me something to that effect."

"Yes; I know him slightly. He has been up here once or twice."

"Well, you're big enough and ugly enough to take care of yourself. He's not what I should call exactly a healthy sort of Johnny, though, no doubt, he's very clever, and all that. But you'll soon find out for yourself. Lee is all right; he's a very decent little fellow. Well, so long, old chap! I row Mullins for the Vice-Chancellor's pot on Wednesday week, so mind you come down, in case I don't see you before."

Bovine Smith laid down his pipe and turned stolidly to his books once more. But with all the will in the world, he found it very hard to keep his mind upon his work. It would slip away to brood upon the man beneath him, and upon the little mystery which hung round his chambers. Then his thoughts turned to this singular attack of which Hastie had spoken, and to the grudge which Bellingham was said to owe to the object of it. The two ideas would persist in rising together in his mind, as though there were some close and intimate connection between them. And yet the suspicion was so dim and vague that it could not be put down in words.

"Confound the chap!" cried Smith, as he shied his book on pathology across the room. "He has spoiled my night's reading, and that's reason enough, if there were no other, why I should steer clear of him in the future."

For ten days the medical student confined himself so closely to his studies that he neither saw nor heard anything of either of the men beneath him. At the hours when Bellingham had been accustomed to visit him, he took care to sport his oak, and though he more than once heard a knocking at his outer door, he resolutely refused to answer it. One afternoon, however, he was descending the stairs when, just as he was passing it, Bellingham's door flew open, and young Monkhouse Lee came out with his eyes sparkling and a dark flush of anger upon his olive cheeks. Close at his heels followed Bellingham, his fat, unhealthy face all quivering with malignant passion.

"You fool!" he hissed. "You'll be sorry."

"Very likely," cried the other. "Mind what I say. It's off! I won't hear of it!"

"You've promised, anyhow."

"Oh, I'll keep that! I won't speak. But I'd rather little Eva was in her grave. Once for all, it's off. She'll do what I say. We don't want to see you again."

So much Smith could not avoid hearing, but he hurried on, for he had no wish to be involved in their dispute. There had been a serious breach between them, that was clear enough, and Lee was going to cause the engagement with his sister to be broken off. Smith thought of Hastie's comparison of the toad and the dove, and was glad to think that the matter was at an end. Bellingham's face when he was in a passion was not pleasant to look upon. He was not a man to whom an innocent girl could be trusted for life. As he walked, Smith wondered languidly what could have caused the quarrel, and what the promise might be which Bellingham had been so anxious that Monkhouse Lee should keep.

It was the day of the sculling match between Hastie and Mullins, and a stream of men were making their way down to the banks of the Isis. A May sun was shining brightly, and the yellow path was barred with the black shadows of tall elm-trees. On either side the grey colleges lay back from the road, the hoary old mothers of minds looking out from their high, mullioned windows at the tide of young life which swept so merrily past them. Black-clad tutors, prim officials, pale, reading men, brown-faced, straw-hatted young athletes in white sweaters or many-coloured blazers, all were hurrying towards the blue, winding river which curves through the Oxford meadows.

Abercrombie Smith, with the intuition of an old oarsman, chose his position at the point where he knew that the struggle, if there were a struggle, would come. Far off he heard the hum which announced the start, the gathering roar of the approach, the thunder of running feet, and the shouts of the men in the boats beneath him. A spray of half-clad, deep-breathing runners shot past him, and craning over their shoulders, he saw Hastie pulling a steady thirty-six, while his opponent, with a jerky forty, was a good boat's length behind him. Smith gave a cheer for his friend, and pulling out his watch, was starting off again for his chambers, when he felt a touch upon his shoulder, and found that young Monkhouse Lee was beside him.

"I saw you there," he said, in a timid, deprecating way. "I wanted to speak to you, if you could spare me a half-hour. This cottage is mine. I share it with Harrington of King's. Come in and have a cup of tea."

"I must be back presently," said Smith. "I am hard on the grind at present. But I'll come in for a few minutes with pleasure. I wouldn't have come out only Hastie is a friend of mine."

"So he is of mine. Hasn't he a beautiful style? Mullins wasn't in it. But come into the cottage. It's a little den of a place, but it is pleasant to work in during the summer months."

It was a small, square, white building, with green doors and shutters, and a rustic trellis-work porch, standing back some fifty yards from the river's bank. Inside, the main room was roughly fitted up as a study—deal table, unpainted shelves with books, and a few cheap oleographs upon the wall. A kettle sang upon a spirit-stove, and there were tea things upon a tray on the table.

"Try that chair and have a cigarette," said Lee. "Let me pour you out a cup of tea. It's so good of you to come in, for I know that your time is a good deal taken up. I wanted to say to you that, if I were you, I should change my rooms at once."

"Eh?"

Smith sat staring at a lighted match in one hand and his unlit cigarette in the other.

"Yes; it must seem very extraordinary, and the worst of it is that I cannot give my reasons, for I am under a solemn promise—a very solemn promise. But I may go so far as to say that I don't think Bellingham is a very safe man to live near. I intend to camp out here as much as I can for a time."

"Not safe! What do you mean?"

"Ah, that's what I mustn't say. But do take my advice and move your rooms. We had a grand row today. You must have heard us, for you came down the stairs."

"I saw that you had fallen out."

"He's a horrible chap, Smith. That is the only word for him. I have had doubts about him ever since that night when he fainted—you remember, when you came down. I taxed him today, and he told me things that made my hair rise, and wanted me to stand in with him. I'm not straight-laced, but I am a clergyman's son, you know, and I think there are some things which are quite beyond the pale. I only thank God that I found him out before it was too late, for he was to have married into my family."

"This is all very fine, Lee," said Abercrombie Smith curtly. "But either you are saying a great deal too much or a great deal too little."

"I give you a warning."

"If there is real reason for warning, no promise can bind you. If I see a rascal about to blow a place up with dynamite no pledge will stand in my way of preventing him."

"Ah, but I cannot prevent him, and I can do nothing but warn you."

"Without saying what you warn me against."

"Against Bellingham."

"But that is childish. Why should I fear him, or any man?"

"I can't tell you. I can only entreat you to change your rooms. You are in danger where you are. I don't even say that Bellingham would wish to injure you. But it might happen, for he is a dangerous neighbour just now."

"Perhaps I know more than you think," said Smith, looking keenly at the young man's boyish, earnest face. "Suppose I tell you that someone else shares Bellingham's rooms."

Monkhouse Lee sprang from his chair in uncontrollable excitement.

"You know, then?" he gasped.

"A woman."

Lee dropped back again with a groan.

"My lips are sealed," he said. "I must not speak."

"Well, anyhow," said Smith, rising, "it is not likely that I should allow myself to be frightened out of rooms which suit me very nicely. It would be a little too feeble for me to move out all my goods and chattels because you say that Bellingham might in some unexplained way do me an injury.

I think that I'll just take my chance, and stay where I am, and as I see that it's nearly five o'clock, I must ask you to excuse me."

He bade the young student adieu in a few curt words, and made his way homeward through the sweet spring evening, feeling half-ruffled, half-amused, as any other strong, unimaginative man might who has been menaced by a vague and shadowy danger.

There was one little indulgence which Abercrombie Smith always allowed himself, however closely his work might press upon him. Twice a week, on the Tuesday and the Friday, it was his invariable custom to walk over to Farlingford, the residence of Doctor Plumptree Peterson, situated about a mile and a half out of Oxford. Peterson had been a close friend of Smith's elder brother, Francis, and as he was a bachelor, fairly well-to-do, with a good cellar and a better library, his house was a pleasant goal for a man who was in need of a brisk walk. Twice a week, then, the medical student would swing out there along the dark country roads and spend a pleasant hour in Peterson's comfortable study, discussing, over a glass of old port, the gossip of the varsity or the latest developments of medicine or of surgery.

On the day which followed his interview with Monkhouse Lee, Smith shut up his books at a quarter past eight, the hour when he usually started for his friend's house. As he was leaving his room, however, his eyes chanced to fall upon one of the books which Bellingham had lent him, and his conscience pricked him for not having returned it. However repellent the man might be, he should not be treated with discourtesy. Taking the book, he walked downstairs and knocked at his neighbour's door. There was no answer; but on turning the handle he found that it was unlocked. Pleased at the thought of avoiding an interview, he stepped inside, and placed the book with his card upon the table.

The lamp was turned half down, but Smith could see the details of the room plainly enough. It was all much as he had seen it before—the frieze, the animal-headed gods, the hanging crocodile, and the table littered over with papers and dried leaves. The mummy case stood upright against the wall, but the mummy itself was missing. There was no sign of any second occupant of the room, and he felt as he withdrew that he had probably done Bellingham an injustice. Had he a guilty secret to preserve, he would hardly leave his door open so that all the world might enter.

The spiral stair was as black as pitch, and Smith was slowly making his way down its irregular steps, when he was suddenly conscious that something had passed him in the darkness. There was a faint sound, a whiff of air, a light brushing past his elbow, but so slight that he could scarcely be certain of it. He stopped and listened, but the wind was rustling among the ivy outside, and he could hear nothing else.

"Is that you, Styles?" he shouted.

There was no answer, and all was still behind him. It must have been a sudden gust of air, for there were crannies and cracks in the old turret. And yet he could almost have sworn that he heard a footfall by his very side. He had emerged into the quadrangle, still turning the matter over in his head, when a man came running swiftly across the smooth-cropped lawn.

"Is that you, Smith?"

"Hullo, Hastie!"

"For God's sake come at once! Young Lee is drowned! Here's Harrington of King's with the news. The doctor is out. You'll do, but come along at once. There may be life in him."

"Have you brandy?"

"No."

"I'll bring some. There's a flask on my table."

Smith bounded up the stairs, taking three at a time, seized the flask, and was rushing down with it, when, as he passed Bellingham's room, his eyes fell upon something which left him gasping and staring upon the landing.

The door, which he had closed behind him, was now open, and right in front of him, with the lamp-light shining upon it, was the mummy case. Three minutes ago it had been empty. He could swear to that. Now it framed the lank body of its horrible occupant, who stood, grim and stark, with his black, shrivelled face towards the door. The form was lifeless and inert, but it seemed to Smith as he gazed that there still lingered a lurid spark of vitality, some faint sign of consciousness in the little eyes which lurked in the depths of the hollow sockets. So astounded and shaken was he that he had forgotten his errand, and was still staring at the lean, sunken figure when the voice of his friend below recalled him to himself.

"Come on, Smith!" he shouted. "It's life and death, you know. Hurry up! Now, then," he added, as the medical student reappeared, "let us do a sprint. It is well under a mile, and we should do it in five minutes. A human life is better worth running for than a pot."

Neck and neck they dashed through the darkness, and did not pull up until panting and spent, they had reached the little cottage by the river. Young Lee, limp and dripping like a broken water-plant, was stretched upon the sofa, the green scum of the river upon his black hair, and a fringe of white foam upon his leaden-hued lips. Beside him knelt his fellow-student, Harrington, endeavouring to chafe some warmth back into his rigid limbs.

"I think there's life in him," said Smith, with his hand to the lad's side. "Put your watch glass to his lips. Yes, there's dimming on it. You take one arm, Hastie. Now work it as I do, and we'll soon pull him round."

For ten minutes they worked in silence, inflating and depressing the chest of the unconscious man. At the end of that time a shiver ran through his body, his lips trembled, and he opened his eyes. The three students burst out into an irrepressible cheer.

"Wake up, old chap. You've frightened us quite enough."

"Have some brandy. Take a sip from the flask."

"He's all right now," said his companion Harrington. "Heavens, what a fright I got! I was reading here, and he had gone out for a stroll as far as the river, when I heard a scream and a splash. Out I ran, and by the time I could find him and fish him out, all life seemed to have gone. Then Simpson couldn't get a doctor, for he has a game-leg, and I had to run, and I don't know what I'd have done without you fellows. That's right, old chap. Sit up."

Monkhouse Lee had raised himself on his hands, and looked wildly about him.

"What's up?" he asked. "I've been in the water. Ah, yes; I remember."

A look of fear came into his eyes, and he sank his face into his hands.

"How did you fall in?"

"I didn't fall in."

"How then?"

"I was thrown in. I was standing by the bank, and something from behind picked me up like a feather and hurled me in. I heard nothing, and I saw nothing. But I know what it was, for all that."

"And so do I," whispered Smith.

Lee looked up with a quick glance of surprise.

"You've learned, then?" he said. "You remember the advice I gave you?"

"Yes, and I begin to think that I shall take it."

"I don't know what the deuce you fellows are talking about," said Hastie, "but I think, if I were you, Harrington, I should get Lee to bed at once. It will be time enough to discuss the why and the wherefore when he is a little stronger. I think, Smith, you and I can leave him alone now. I am walking back to college; if you are coming in that direction, we can have a chat."

But it was little chat that they had upon their homeward path. Smith's mind was too full of the incidents of the evening, the absence of the mummy from his neighbour's rooms, the step that passed him on the stair, the reappearance—the extraordinary, inexplicable reappearance of the grisly thing—and then this attack upon Lee, corresponding so closely to the previous outrage upon another man against whom Bellingham bore a grudge. All this settled in his thoughts, together with the many little incidents which had previously turned him against his neighbour, and the singular circumstances under which he was first called in to him. What had been a dim suspicion, a vague, fantastic conjecture, had suddenly taken form, and stood out in his mind as a grim fact, a thing not to be denied. And yet, how monstrous it was! how unheard of! how entirely beyond all bounds of human experience. An impartial judge, or even the friend who walked by his side, would simply tell him that his eyes had deceived him, that the mummy had been there all the time, that young Lee had tumbled into the river as any other man tumbles into a river, and the blue pill was the best thing for a disordered liver. He felt that he would have said as much if the positions had been reversed. And yet he could swear that Bellingham was a murderer at heart, and that he wielded a weapon such as no man had ever used in all the grim history of crime.

Hastie had branched off to his rooms with a few crisp and emphatic comments upon his friend's unsociability, and Abercrombie Smith crossed the quadrangle to his corner turret with a strong feeling of repulsion for his chambers and their associations. He would take Lee's advice, and move his quarters as soon as possible, for how could a man study when his ear was ever straining for every murmur or footstep in the room below? He observed, as he crossed over the lawn, that the light was still shining in Bellingham's window, and as he passed up the staircase the door opened, and the man himself looked out at him. With his fat, evil face he was like some bloated spider fresh from the weaving of his poisonous web.

"Good evening," said he. "Won't you come in?"

"No," cried Smith fiercely.

"No? You are as busy as ever? I wanted to ask you about Lee. I was sorry to hear that there was a rumour that something was amiss with him."

His features were grave, but there was the gleam of a hidden laugh in his eyes as he spoke. Smith saw it, and he could have knocked him down for it.

"You'll be sorrier still to hear that Monkhouse Lee is doing very well, and is out of all danger," he answered. "Your hellish tricks have not come off this time. Oh, you needn't try to brazen it out. I know all about it."

Bellingham took a step back from the angry student, and half-closed the door as if to protect himself.

"You are mad," he said. "What do you mean? Do you assert that I had anything to do with Lee's accident?"

"Yes," thundered Smith. "You and that bag of bones behind you; you worked it between you. I tell you what it is, Master B., they have given up burning folk like you, but we still keep a hangman, and, by George! if any man in this college meets his death while you are here, I'll have you up, and if you don't swing for it, it won't be my fault. You'll find that your filthy Egyptian tricks won't answer in England."

"You're a raving lunatic," said Bellingham.

"All right. You just remember what I say, for you'll find that I'll be better than my word."

The door slammed, and Smith went fuming up to his chamber, where he locked the door upon the inside, and spent half the night in smoking his old briar and brooding over the strange events of the evening.

Next morning Abercrombie Smith heard nothing of his neighbour, but Harrington called upon him in the afternoon to say that Lee was almost himself again. All day Smith stuck fast to his work, but in the evening he determined to pay the visit to his friend Doctor Peterson upon which he had started the night before. A good walk and a friendly chat would be welcome to his jangled nerves.

Bellingham's door was shut as he passed, but glancing back when he was some distance from the turret, he saw his neighbour's head at the window outlined against the lamp-light, his face pressed apparently against the glass as he gazed out into the darkness. It was a blessing to be away from all contact with him, if but for a few hours, and Smith stepped out briskly, and breathed the soft spring air into his lungs. The half-moon lay in the west between two Gothic pinnacles, and threw upon the silvered street a dark tracery from the stonework above. There was a brisk breeze, and light, fleecy clouds drifted swiftly across the sky. Old's was on the very border of the town, and in five minutes Smith found himself beyond the houses and between the hedges of a May-scented, Oxfordshire lane.

It was a lonely and little-frequented road which led to his friend's house. Early as it was, Smith did not meet a single soul upon his way. He walked briskly along until he came to the avenue gate, which opened into the long, gravel drive leading up to Farlingford. In front of him he could see the cosy, red light of the windows glimmering through the foliage. He stood with his hand upon the iron latch of the swinging gate, and he glanced back at the road along which he had come. Something was coming swiftly down it.

It moved in the shadow of the hedge, silently and furtively, a dark, crouching figure, dimly visible against the black background. Even as he gazed back at it, it had lessened its distance by twenty paces, and was fast closing upon him. Out of the darkness he had a glimpse of a scraggy neck, and of two eyes that will ever haunt him in his dreams. He turned, and with a cry of terror he ran for his life up the avenue. There were the red lights, the signals of safety, almost within a stone's-throw of him. He was a famous runner, but never had he run as he ran that night.

The heavy gate had swung into place behind him but he heard it dash open again before his pursuer. As he rushed madly and wildly through the night, he could hear a swift, dry patter behind him, and could see, as he threw back a glance, that this horror was bounding like a tiger at his heels, with blazing eyes and one stringy arm out-thrown. Thank God, the door was ajar. He could see the thin bar of light which shot from the lamp in the hall. Nearer yet sounded the clatter from behind. He heard a hoarse gurgling at his very shoulder. With a shriek he flung himself against the door, slammed and bolted it behind him, and sank half-fainting on to the hall chair.

"My goodness, Smith, what's the matter?" asked Peterson, appearing at the door of his study.

"Give me some brandy."

Peterson disappeared, and came rushing out again with a glass and a decanter.

"You need it," he said, as his visitor drank off what he poured out for him. "Why, man, you are as white as a cheese."

Smith laid down his glass, rose up, and took a deep breath.

"I am my own man again now," said he. "I was never so unmanned before. But, with your leave, Peterson, I will sleep here tonight, for I don't think I could face that road again except by daylight. It's weak, I know, but I can't help it."

Peterson looked at his visitor with a very questioning eye.

"Of course you shall sleep here if you wish. I'll tell Mrs. Burney to make up the spare bed. Where are you off to now?"

"Come up with me to the window that overlooks the door. I want you to see what I have seen."

They went up to the window of the upper hall whence they could look down upon the approach to the house. The drive and the fields on either side lay quiet and still, bathed in the peaceful moonlight.

"Well, really, Smith," remarked Peterson, "it is well that I know you to be an abstemious man. What in the world can have frightened you?"

"I'll tell you presently. But where can it have gone? Ah, now, look, look! See the curve of the road just beyond your gate."

"Yes, I see; you needn't pinch my arm off. I saw someone pass. I should say a man, rather thin, apparently, and tall, very tall. But what of him? And what of yourself? You are still shaking like an aspen leaf."

"I have been within hand-grip of the devil, that's all. But come down to your study, and I shall tell you the whole story."

He did so. Under the cheery lamp-light with a glass of wine on the table beside him, and the portly form and florid face of his friend in front, he narrated, in their order, all the events, great and small, which had formed so singular a chain, from the night on which he had found Bellingham fainting in front of the mummy case until this horrid experience of an hour ago.

"There now," he said as he concluded, "that's the whole, black business. It is monstrous and incredible, but it is true."

Doctor Plumptree Peterson sat for some time in silence with a very puzzled expression upon his face.

"I never heard of such a thing in my life, never!" he said at last. "You have told me the facts. Now tell me your inferences."

"You can draw your own."

"But I should like to hear yours. You have thought over the matter, and I have not."

"Well, it must be a little vague in detail, but the main points seem to me to be clear enough. This fellow Bellingham, in his

Eastern studies, has got hold of some infernal secret by which a mummy—or possibly only this particular mummy—can be temporarily brought to life. He was trying this disgusting business on the night when he fainted. No doubt the sight of the creature moving had shaken his nerve, even though he had expected it. You remember that almost the first words he said were to call out upon himself as a fool. Well, he got more hardened afterwards, and carried the matter through without fainting. The vitality which he could put into it was evidently only a passing thing, for I have seen it continually in its case as dead as this table. He has some elaborate process, I fancy, by which he brings the thing to pass. Having done it, he naturally bethought him that he might use the creature as an agent. It has intelligence and it has strength. For some purpose he took Lee into his confidence; but Lee, like a decent Christian, would have nothing to do with such a business. Then they had a row, and Lee vowed that he would tell his sister of Bellingham's true character. Bellingham's game was to prevent him, and he nearly managed it, by setting this creature of his on his track. He had already tried its powers upon another man—Norton—towards whom he had a grudge. It is the merest chance that he has not two murders upon his soul. Then, when I taxed him with the matter, he had the strongest reasons for wishing to get me out of the way before I could convey my knowledge to anyone else. He got his chance when I went out, for he knew my habits and where I was bound for. I have had a narrow shave, Peterson, and it is mere luck that you didn't find me on your doorstep in the morning. I'm not a nervous man as a rule, and I never thought to have the fear of death put upon me as it was tonight."

"My dear boy, you take the matter too seriously," said his companion. "Your nerves are out of order with your work, and you make too much of it. How could such a thing as this stride about the streets of Oxford, even at night, without being seen?"

"It has been seen. There is quite a scare in the town about an escaped ape, as they imagine the creature to be. It is the talk of the place."

"Well, it's a striking chain of events. And yet, my dear fellow, you must allow that each incident in itself is capable of a more natural explanation?"

"What! even my adventure of tonight?"

"Certainly. You come out with your nerves all unstrung, and your head full of this theory of yours. Some gaunt, half-famished tramp steals after you, and seeing you run, is emboldened to pursue you. Your fears and imagination do the rest."

"It won't do, Peterson; it won't do."

"And again, in the instance of your finding the mummy case empty, and then a few moments later with an occupant, you know that it was lamp-light, that the lamp was half turned down, and that you had no special reason to look hard at the case. It is quite possible that you may have overlooked the creature in the first instance."

"No, no; it is out of the question."

"And then Lee may have fallen into the river, and Norton been garrotted. It is certainly a formidable indictment that you have against Bellingham; but if you were to place it before a police magistrate, he would simply laugh in your face."

"I know he would. That is why I mean to take the matter into my own hands."

"Eh?"

"Yes; I feel that a public duty rests upon me, and besides, I must do it for my own safety, unless I choose to allow myself to be hunted by this beast out of the college, and that would be a little too feeble. I have quite made up my mind what I shall do. And first of all, may I use your paper and pens for an hour?"

"Most certainly. You will find all that you want upon that side-table."

Abercrombie Smith sat down before a sheet of foolscap, and for an hour, and then for a second hour his pen travelled swiftly over it. Page after page was finished and tossed aside while his friend leaned back in his armchair, looking across at him with patient curiosity. At last, with an exclamation of satisfaction, Smith sprang to his feet, gathered his papers up into order, and laid the last one upon Peterson's desk.

"Kindly sign this as a witness," he said.

"A witness? Of what?"

"Of my signature, and of the date. The date is the most important. Why, Peterson, my life might hang upon it."

"My dear Smith, you are talking wildly. Let me beg you to go to bed."

"On the contrary, I never spoke so deliberately in my life. And I will promise to go to bed the moment you have signed it."

"But what is it?"

"It is a statement of all that I have been telling you tonight. I wish you to witness it."

"Certainly," said Peterson, signing his name under that of his companion. "There you are! But what is the idea?"

"You will kindly retain it, and produce it in case I am arrested."

"Arrested? For what?"

"For murder. It is quite on the cards. I wish to be ready for every event. There is only one course open to me, and I am determined to take it."

"For Heaven's sake, don't do anything rash!"

"Believe me, it would be far more rash to adopt any other course. I hope that we won't need to bother you, but it will ease my mind to know that you have this statement of my motives. And now I am ready to take your advice and to go to roost, for I want to be at my best in the morning."

Abercrombie Smith was not an entirely pleasant man to have as an enemy. Slow and easy-tempered, he was formidable when driven to action. He brought to every purpose in life the same deliberate resoluteness which had distinguished him as a scientific student. He had laid his studies aside for a day, but he intended that the day should not be wasted. Not a word did he say to his host as to his plans, but by nine o'clock he was well on his way to Oxford.

In the High Street he stopped at Clifford's, the gun-maker's, and bought a heavy revolver, with a box of central-fire cartridges. Six of them he slipped into the chambers, and half-cocking the weapon, placed it in the pocket of his coat. He then made his way to Hastie's rooms, where the big oarsman was lounging over his breakfast, with the Sporting Times propped up against the coffee-pot.

"Hullo! What's up?" he asked. "Have some coffee?"

"No, thank you. I want you to come with me, Hastie, and do what I ask you."

"Certainly, my boy."

"And bring a heavy stick with you."

"Hullo!" Hastie stared. "Here's a hunting crop that would fell an ox."

"One other thing. You have a box of amputating knives. Give me the longest of them."

"There you are. You seem to be fairly on the war trail. Anything else?"

"No; that will do." Smith placed the knife inside his coat, and led the way to the quadrangle. "We are neither of us chickens, Hastie," said he. "I think I can do this job alone, but I take you as a precaution. I am going to have a little talk with Bellingham. If I have only him to deal with, I won't, of course, need you. If I shout, however, up you come, and lam out with your whip as hard as you can lick. Do you understand?"

"All right. I'll come if I hear you bellow."

"Stay here, then. I may be a little time, but don't budge until I come down."

"I'm a fixture."

Smith ascended the stairs, opened Bellingham's door and stepped in. Bellingham was seated behind his table, writing. Beside him, among his litter of strange possessions, towered the mummy case, with its sale number 249 still stuck upon its front, and its hideous occupant stiff and stark within it. Smith looked very deliberately round him, closed the door, and then, stepping across to the fireplace, struck a match and set the fire alight. Bellingham sat staring, with amazement and rage upon his bloated face.

"Well, really now, you make yourself at home," he gasped.

Smith sat himself deliberately down, placing his watch upon the table, drew out his pistol, cocked it, and laid it in his lap.

Then he took the long amputating knife from his bosom, and threw it down in front of Bellingham.

"Now, then," said he, "just get to work and cut up that mummy."

"Oh, is that it?" said Bellingham with a sneer.

"Yes, that is it. They tell me that the law can't touch you. But I have a law that will set matters straight. If in five minutes you have not set to work, I swear by the God who made me that I will put a bullet through your brain!"

"You would murder me?"

Bellingham had half-risen, and his face was the colour of putty.

"Yes."

"And for what?"

"To stop your mischief. One minute has gone."

"But what have I done?"

"I know and you know."

"This is mere bullying."

"Two minutes are gone."

"But you must give reasons. You are a madman—a dangerous madman. Why should I destroy my own property? It is a valuable mummy."

"You must cut it up, and you must burn it."

"I will do no such thing."

"Four minutes are gone."

Smith took up the pistol and he looked towards Bellingham with an inexorable face. As the second-hand stole round, he raised his hand, and the finger twitched upon the trigger.

"There! there! I'll do it!" screamed Bellingham.

In frantic haste he caught up the knife and hacked at the figure of the mummy, ever glancing round to see the eye and the weapon of his terrible visitor bent upon him. The creature crackled and snapped under every stab of the keen blade. A thick, yellow dust rose up from it. Spices and dried essences rained down upon the floor. Suddenly, with a rending crack, its backbone snapped asunder, and it fell, a brown heap of sprawling limbs, upon the floor.

"Now into the fire!" said Smith.

The flames leaped and roared as the dried and tinder-like debris was piled upon it. The little room was like the stoke-hole of a steamer and the sweat ran down the faces of the two men; but still the one stooped and worked, while the other sat watching him with a set face. A thick, fat smoke oozed out from the fire, and a heavy smell of burned resin and singed hair filled the air. In a quarter of an hour a few charred and brittle sticks were all that was left of Lot No. 249.

"Perhaps that will satisfy you," snarled Bellingham, with hate and fear in his little grey eyes as he glanced back at his tormentor.

"No; I must make a clean sweep of all your materials. We must have no more devil's tricks. In with all these leaves! They may have something to do with it."

"And what now?" asked Bellingham, when the leaves also had been added to the blaze.

"Now the roll of papyrus which you had on the table that night. It is in that drawer, I think."

"No, no," shouted Bellingham. "Don't burn that! Why, man, you don't know what you do. It is unique; it contains wisdom which is nowhere else to be found."

"Out with it!"

"But look here, Smith, you can't really mean it. I'll share the knowledge with you. I'll teach you all that is in it. Or, stay, let me only copy it before you burn it!"

Smith stepped forward and turned the key in the drawer. Taking out the yellow, curled roll of paper, he threw it into the fire, and pressed it down with his heel. Bellingham screamed, and grabbed at it; but Smith pushed him back and stood over it until it was reduced to a formless, grey ash.

"Now, Master B.," said he, "I think I have pretty well drawn your teeth. You'll hear from me again, if you return to your old tricks. And now good morning, for I must go back to my studies."

And such is the narrative of Abercrombie Smith as to the singular events which occurred in Old College, Oxford, in the spring of '84. As Bellingham left the university immediately afterwards, and was last heard of in the Soudan, there is no one who can contradict his statement. But the wisdom of men is small, and the ways of Nature are strange, and who shall put a bound to the dark things which may be found by those who seek for them?

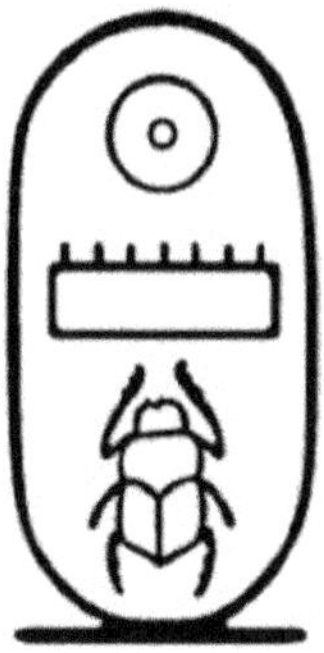

THE END

# The Authors

**"The Mummy's Foot"** by Pierre Jules Théophile Gautier (France, 1811–1872) was originally published in the magazine *Musée des Familles* in 1840. "*Le Pied de momie*" was later translated from French by Lafcadio Hearn and published in a collection of six of Gautier's fantasy short stories called *One of Cleopatra's Nights and Other Fantastic Romances* in 1882. Gautier's work as an artist, poet, playwright, and novelist informed his career as a critic of dance, art, theater and literature.

**"After Three Thousand Years"** by Jane Goodwin Austin (Massachusetts, 1831–1894) was published in *Putnam's Magazine* in 1868. Along with Louisa May Alcott, she was lifelong friends with a group of fellow New England authors including Nathaniel Hawthorne and Ralph Waldo Emerson. A Daughter of the American Revolution and a descendant of Pilgrims, the most popular of Austin's many books and short stories were filled with finely written details of the early American, pre-Colonial and Revolutionary War eras.

**"Lost in a Pyramid, or the Mummy's Curse"** by Louisa May Alcott (Massachusetts, 1832–1888) was likely written in late 1868, the same time as the publication of the first book of her most famous work, the semi-autobiographical two-volume novel *Little Women*. "Lost in a Pyramid" was published in Frank Leslie's *The New World Magazine* in 1869. A fierce abolitionist and crusader against traditional gender roles in life, Alcott is buried in Sleepy Hollow Cemetery in Concord, MA alongside her friends and colleagues Emerson, Thoreau, and Hawthorne.

**"Lot No. 249"** by Arthur Ignatius Conan Doyle (Scotland, 1859–1930) was published in *Harper's Magazine* in 1892. It was reprinted in *Tales of Twilight and the Unseen*, a collection of 12 of his short stories published by John Murray in 1922. With a sensibility unlike his most famous literary creation, the rationalist Sherlock Holmes, the credulous Conan Doyle was a Spiritualist, opening a psychic bookshop in London in 1925.

Lightning Source UK Ltd.
Milton Keynes UK
UKHW011851260619
345095UK00001B/125/P

9 781947 587052